Love You Sober

ANDRÉA JOY

Leah

Deacon

Sad/Hurt

Redemption

Relationship

Copyright © 2022 by Andréa Joy

Cover Design: Dani René at Raven Designs

Editing: Sandra D at One Love Editing

All rights reserved.

No part of this book may be reproduced in any form or by any electronic or mechanical means, including information storage and retrieval systems, without written permission from the author, except for the use of brief quotations in a book review.

ISBN: 978-1-9992413-7-7

Author Note

First and foremost, thank you for taking a chance on Love You Sober. This is not your traditional romance book, but I promise their story does have a HEA ending. You just have to wait a little bit longer for it. It will be hard earned, though, as none of the topics covered in this book have easy fixes.

Second, this book does include some trigger warnings. For the full list, please click on the link *trigger warnings* in the content list.

Please consider leaving a review once you have read Love You Sober. Thank you.

Blurb

The first time I met Deacon Rutherford, the sun didn't shine brighter. It felt like any ordinary day like the ones before it. But it was the day my world had irrevocably changed.

When I came close to dying, he offered me a lifeline.

When I needed a family, he gave me his.

He was selfless and gentle, and everything I'd convinced myself I would never have.

Deacon Rutherford opened a world that had been out of reach to me for a long time. I would be forever grateful to him, but I couldn't rely on him to fight my demons forever.

At some point I would have to face my past. Would his lifeline be enough to keep my walls from crashing? Or would I drown?

Chapter One

L eah

I FLINCHED AS I PUSHED THE NEEDLE INTO A VEIN. YEARS of using, and I still hated that first prick. I pushed the plunger of the rig until it was empty and then untied the torniquet from around my bicep. I capped it and tossed the used rig into the paper bag.

As the drug worked its way through my body, the image of my dad lying dead on the living room carpet faded. The cruel voices of foster families... silent. The pain from years of being used... gone. All that was left was a blissful quiet. I felt my lips curve into a soft smile as my eyes fell closed.

"Hey!" someone yelled. "Hey! You can't be doing that here."

I grumbled and swatted at whatever had poked me in

the arm. I cracked my eyes open to see the attendant standing over me with a long tree branch. That was new.

"You need to leave, or I'm gonna call the cops."

"Hmm. I'm going."

I shifted until I was on my knees and braced my palms on the cold ground to push myself up. My entire body felt so heavy, it was a struggle to keep my eyes open as I staggered to my feet. The attendant yelled something at my back, but I ignored him as I walked across the lot to the sidewalk.

It was an unseasonable warm day in Adelaide, British Columbia, for March. The snow had begun melting the week before, and brown grass was beginning to peek through. I wasn't complaining, though. I had lost my coat sometime between shooting up and now. The memory of handing it to a young girl who looked to be in her early twenties was vague at best. I couldn't decipher whether it was a memory or a dream. *Probably a dream*, I thought. At least I still had the heavy sweater I'd swiped from the donations bin at a women's shelter months ago.

I stuffed my hands in the pockets of the sweater and realized there was something in one of the pockets. I swayed on the sidewalk as I pulled one of my hands out of the pocket to reveal a sandwich. I couldn't remember where I'd gotten it. Probably from the shelter the night before. I was too focused on unwrapping it and not at all paying attention to where I was going when I took a wrong turn and ended up down an alley with no exit.

I took a minute to lean against the brick wall. My limbs were heavy with fatigue, but my mind was blissfully quiet. The feel of the sandwich wrapper sliding through my fingers made me snap my eyes open, and I jerked upright, but it wasn't enough to keep me awake.

I heard their footsteps first. Their snickers and taunts sounded like evil cackles as they entered the alley and blocked me in. They leered at me when I turned to face them. If I hadn't just used, I was sure I would be afraid, but the heaviness holding me down was too strong. My lids drooped as I leaned my head back against the cold, hard surface of the building behind me.

"Leave me alone." I slurred and tried to straighten my shoulders to make myself look more confident. More awake.

There were times in this life when appearing smaller, less threatening, was the right way to go. Most people didn't look at you twice then. This was not one of those times. I knew that if I let them see the fear coiling itself around my heart, they would salivate.

Being five foot three and about a hundred pounds soaking wet, that wasn't all that easy to do.

The taller of the three, and who I assumed was the leader, laughed as he nudged the man to one side and said, "She wants us to leave her alone."

"She can't even hold herself up."

The third man mock pouted, even as he flicked out a switchblade by his side. "Aw, c'mon, babe. We just want your services."

Anger mixed with the fear, and the combination rolled through my veins. I tried to curl my fingers in a tight fist at my side.

"I'm not a whore, and even if I were, you wouldn't be able to afford me." I managed to push myself off the wall but then staggered and shot out a hand to steady myself.

I cringed. That was not the right thing to say if I wanted them to leave me alone.

All three of them snarled, and the other two pulled

out their blades as they drew closer. I swallowed down the bile rising up the back of my throat and took a couple of steps back and immediately groaned in frustration at my own stupidity. In an effort to put more distance between me and the three men, I'd backed up into a corner. If I hadn't truly been caged in before, I was then.

Two of the men took up positions on each side of me, with the leader toe to toe with me. There was a predatory look on his face. My stomach dropped.

I knew that look. I'd seen that look once before. I wasn't going to take it without a fight, though. Not this time. I didn't care that the odds weren't in my favour. My brain was yelling at me to run, but my body refused to listen. I struggled to keep my eyes open longer. Struggled to push through the high.

I gathered all the saliva I could and spat in the man's face. While he was distracted for a moment, I attempted to bring my foot up and kick the guy to my right in the nuts, but the guy on my left grabbed me around my waist and hauled me back before my foot could make contact. It felt like I thrashed and kicked widely, but in reality, I probably looked like a wet noodle. Pathetic.

All that got me were my arms yanked behind my back in a tight grip and a fist to the stomach. I doubled over as far as I could with my arms wrenched back, the sandwich long forgotten as it lay in a deconstructed mess on the ground. I might have been more furious about the loss of a sandwich than being punched in the gut.

"You're going to pay for that," the leader snarled as he backhanded me for my efforts.

My head snapped to the side, and a metallic taste hit my tongue as my lip was split open. I struggled even harder in guy number three's hold. Guy number one grabbed at the sweater and ripped it down the middle, forcing the zipper off its tracks.

"No, please," I cried when he repeated the motion with my shirt, all semblance of confidence gone.

"Shut up, you druggie whore," one of them snapped; I wasn't sure who.

I tried to kick out, but my legs refused to listen. I had hoped to hit one of them hard enough to distract them so that I could make a run for the only exit. All that got me were a couple more fists to the stomach and face.

Then a voice I'd never forget broke through enough for the hits to stop.

[one word that's going to change all...]

"Hey!"

I tensed up at the first sound of his voice, thinking it was another one of their friends coming to join them, but when I turned in the direction of the voice and caught a glimpse of the new man, I knew he could never be associated with thugs like these.

He looked like a superhero standing at the end of the alley, backlit by the early spring sun, however much could be seen over his broad shoulders. He was tall — taller than the leader of this little group.

The man holding my arms let me go to join his two friends as they stood before the newcomer. I took the opportunity to slump back against the wall. My legs shook, and I crumbled to the ground. My face throbbed, and it hurt to breathe. I was pretty sure my ribs weren't broken. I'd had them broken multiple times in the past, and this pain was nothing like that. Probably just bruised, then. My eyes still felt heavy, so I let them droop closed, even as I struggled to watch the confrontation play out before me. Blissful oblivion took over.

"Hey, are you okay?"

I grumbled at having been shook awake. Fuckers

were really messing with my high. I snapped my eyes open at how close the voice sounded and frantically scanned the alley only to see that it was just me and the newcomer. The three men must have taken off, then.

I shook my head. No, I didn't think I was okay. I immediately stopped when the nausea started. Suddenly, the man in front of me morphed into three identical copies.

"Do you need me to call an ambulance?"

I tried to tell him that I didn't want to go to the hospital. I hated doctors. Hated how they looked down at me because of my situation, but I don't think I managed more than a squeak before my eyes rolled to the back of my head, and everything went black.

Chapter Two

L eah

I SCREWED MY EYES SHUT AGAINST THE HARSH LIGHT. Who the hell opened the curtains while someone was still sleeping? I had half a mind to bitch at one of the residents to close the damn curtains. It must have still been too early for wake-up calls at the shelter, or one of the workers would've come around already.

That's when I noticed the softness of the mattress beneath me. As in, it was too soft and not something the shelter would've sprung for. They had too many beds and not enough funds to purchase a mattress this soft and comfortable. I snuggled deeper under the covers and wished for sleep to come back. If this was a dream, I wanted it to last a little longer.

The smell of coffee reiterated that I very well could

be dreaming. It was the press of a cold nose against my arm and a quiet *meow* that disproved the thought.

Unease tightened my gut as I cracked open an eye. Unfamiliar blue curtains stared back at me while they tried to block the ray of early morning sun. What the fuck did I do last night? Where was I?

I scrambled up and sat back against the headboard with the duvet drawn up to my chin. A little ball of orange fur bolted off the bed and behind a chair at the sudden movement.

I winced and cursed at the pain in my side. I peeked under the covers. Patterns of black, blue, and yellow decorated the expanse of my stomach. I still had my pants on, but my sweater was gone, leaving me in only a bra.

The pain helped to slowly bring back the events of yesterday. Shooting up behind the gas station. The incident in the alley with the three men. The newcomer who chased them off. Nodding out. I breathed out a painful sigh of relief that someone had been able to chase them off before things escalated.

I peeled the duvet back and carefully swung my legs over the edge of the bed. I sat there for a while, trying to catch my breath and get the motivation to stand. I had half a mind to lie back down and give back in to sleep.

I yawned, looked up and stared at my reflection in the mirror across the room. My brown hair looked dull and mussed. Dark circles surrounded my once bright, brown eyes. Except for the bruises, my skin looked ghostly. Shame bloomed in my chest.

Everything I had ever been told over the last several years came flying back.

You're worthless.
What did you expect?

You had it coming.

I knew the words were weapons meant to hurt with untruths, but that didn't mean they hadn't sunken their claws in deep. I needed another hit and wondered how far I was to downtown. I tried standing up from the bed, but the burden of judgements coupled with the unknown of what awaited me on the other side of the door weighed me down.

"Just get it over with it," I murmured to myself as I tried again. This time, I made it to my feet. The need to use propelling me forward more than anything.

I winced and gingerly pressed my fingertips to the ugly bruise. I was no stranger to physical pain, but I'd at least had somewhere warm to sleep and something warm to eat back then. Now, it was just the occasional shelter and whatever I could find in the dumpsters behind grocery stores at night. The first time I resigned myself to dumpster diving, I was surprised at the amount of packaged food grocery stores threw out. Why not donate them to the shelters in town? It was such a waste, but it was exactly what I needed at the time.

Not wanting to overstay my welcome, I swiped a black zip-up hoodie from a chair in the corner of the room beside the door and slipped it on. I'd have to find some way of thanking him later for helping me in that alley and apologize for taking his clothes. Assuming that he was the one who'd brought me to this place. I sincerely hoped so.

I eased the door open as silently as I could and poked my head out. The room was at the end of a short hallway, but I couldn't see anything from here except for a door across the way, which was open, exposing a bathroom.

I yawned again. *Fuck, how long had it been since the last time I used?*

A jazz melody played quietly from overhead speakers placed in the ceiling throughout the apartment, but other than that, the house was quiet.

On tiptoes, I crept out of the room and down the hallway. With any luck, he'd left me alone, and I'd be long gone by the time he got back. I stopped short at the end of the hall. In front of me was one giant open space consisting of a living room and kitchen. I would've given anything to walk over to the big leather couch and sink into it while pulling the heavy throw blanket over myself. I was freezing.

But that's not what stopped me. Standing in the kitchen, in a pair of painted-on jeans and a white T-shirt, was the newcomer from the alley.

His back was to me, so I couldn't get a good look at him. But he was at least six feet tall with a solid build. His shoulder muscles flexed as he stirred something on the stove. If he heard me creeping down the hallway, he didn't say anything.

I sucked in a quiet breath and tiptoed my way behind the couch and over to the front door. I'd made it about five feet away when his deep voice stopped me.

"Do you want some breakfast before you take off?"

I let out the breath I held, and my shoulders dropped back down.

"What am I doing here?" I asked, not moving from my place between the couch and front door.

He went about collecting plates from the overhead cupboards and eggs from the fridge. It smelled delicious. My stomach growled.

"Well," he replied, "I wasn't about to leave you in that alley by yourself."

"You could've taken me to the hospital."

Why the hell was I arguing with this man? I should've been grateful that he hadn't left me unconscious for those men to find.

"You asked me not to before you lost consciousness." He glanced quickly over his shoulder at me. There was something unreadable in his expression before he turned away again. "Take a seat. Breakfast is almost ready. How do you like your eggs?"

I tentatively moved away from the front door and toward the kitchen. "S-scrambled," I managed through another yawn.

"Tired?"

I shook my head feeling my cheeks heat. Yawning was one of my ticks. A tell that if I didn't get more drugs and soon, I'd start going through some serious withdrawal.

I was still confused as to why a stranger would stop to help me. Most people usually just kept their heads down and continued on their way if they heard someone calling for help. I had given up hope for humanity a long time ago.

"Smells good," I added on when he began cracking the eggs into the warm pan.

While he continued making us breakfast, I took my first opportunity to really study him. He wasn't attractive in the traditional sense, I guessed. He was solid with a little bit of a belly from what I could see over the counter that separated us. His hair was dark, cropped short to the scalp with little bits of grey peppered throughout. The grey continued into the neatly trimmed scruff that lined his sharp jaw.

"Thank you," I managed as my fingers toyed with the napkin holder on the counter, white napkins stacked inside. My voice was barely above a whisper; I was surprised he even heard it.

He hummed. "It's just breakfast."

He plated the food, turned off the stove, and placed two identical plates on the bar countertop, one in front of me. I couldn't even remember when the last time was that I'd eaten this much food.

"No. Well, yes, thank you for this too." I motioned to the plate in front of me. "But I meant yesterday. Thank you for stepping in. If you hadn't..." My voice trailed off, and I looked away, embarrassed. I didn't want to see the pity that I was sure would be present in his expression.

I tried not to flinch when a warm, calloused hand enveloped mine on the counter. He'd barely touched me before he pulled away again. Touch wasn't something that was always welcomed when you'd been living on the streets for as long as I had because most of the time, it was done with malicious intent. I'd only just met this man, didn't know anything about him, and yet I felt the loss of his brief touch like a chasm.

I tried not to let the wiggle of guilt take hold and failed. I wanted to tell him that it wasn't his touch that made me flinch, but that I wasn't used to it not being accompanied by pain.

He cleared his throat before asking, "Did you know any of them?"

I lifted a shoulder in a sort of shrug while I fought back another yawn. "No, but it's not uncommon. Not for someone like me."

"Someone like you?" he asked.

I lifted my head and met his eyes for the first time and noticed how green they were in the morning light. "An addict. Homeless." I confessed the last part under my breath and hoped he hadn't heard it, but from the tic in his jaw, I knew he had. I just didn't know if that tic was because of my confession about being a drug addict or about being homeless, or maybe both. My knee started bouncing under the counter. I needed to get out of here.

Chapter Three

D eacon

I'D JUST LEFT FROM HELPING A COUPLE OF MY BROTHERS set up for a barbeque at the local shelter when something told me to look down the alleyway that separated a nightclub and a bar. What I saw made my stomach drop and anger flood my veins. I'd never been a fighter in my life, except for my brief stint in the military, but I wished I hadn't let those men off as easily as I had. I should've made it so they had to crawl out of that alley instead of run like they did.

Cowards.

It looked like she was in a lot of pain but trying to play it off like it was nothing as she sat at my dining room table. And the fact that she couldn't stop yawning made me worry and wonder when was the last time she'd had any decent amount of sleep.

"Let me help you."

I had no idea why those words left my lips, but I felt like I needed to put the offer out there. I didn't know the first thing about being a drug addict or being homeless, but even barely knowing this woman, I already felt protective over her. Plus, if I could help her, then I could help others as well. I wasn't naïve enough to believe that helping a few addicts would put a dent in eliminating the overdose pandemic, but it had to be better than doing nothing.

She looked at me skeptically, and I didn't blame her. I was a stranger offering her help. She had no way of knowing that I wouldn't finish what it seemed those men in the alley had started. She had no reason to trust me. Her next question wasn't exactly a surprise.

"Why? You don't know me."

"True," I said. "But I wanted to offer. If you wanted help, the offer is there."

"How? What makes you think you can help more than the shelters or treatment centres?"

I placed the napkin I held in my hand on my plate and pushed the entire thing away before leaning back in my seat and facing her. "I don't. I don't have the first clue as to what to do, but one of my brothers is a paramedic and another one a doctor. We can go to my cabin in the mountains for however long it takes."

I'd need to check in with a couple of the guys who work for me, but I was confident that they could handle the current projects just fine without me for a few weeks.

I had no idea why words kept spilling from my lips. It *means you're a good person.* was like the filter that existed between my thoughts and my mouth was no longer working.

She squirmed in her seat and avoided eye contact

like she was worried if I saw her eyes for even a split second, I'd be able to read her completely.

When she still hadn't responded after a few minutes, I added, "I'll never judge you…"

"Leah," she supplied when I trailed off.

I smiled. "Deacon."

She returned my smile and dipped her chin in a pseudo new greeting now that we knew the other's name. "So, a mountain cabin, huh?"

"Nobody around for miles. It's the perfect place for privacy."

"Or to get murdered."

I grinned. "If I wanted to kill you, I wouldn't have brought you to my home, where there are pictures of my family everywhere." I gestured to the photo wall my sister had put up a few weeks after I moved in.

"Or," she started with a playful smile, her knee paused its incessant bouncing, "that's exactly what you would do because I'd be dead and wouldn't be able to identify you even if I wanted to."

"Nah, that's too much fucking work. To move a body from the city to the mountains. I don't have time for that shit."

Our gazes locked, and we stared at each other for several moments before breaking out in laughter.

After a while, the laughter died down, and we sat awkwardly at the counter. Leah began fiddling with the cuffs of the sleeves of the sweater I had left on the chair in the bedroom. Her dark brown hair fell forward, curtaining her face from view. My fingers twitched with the need to push it back so I could glimpse those dark eyes again. Eyes that held a story of turmoil and pain. Things I wanted to heal.

I could hear my family's voices now.

You can't fix everybody, Deacon.
Not everyone wants help.
Don't stick your nose where it doesn't belong, bro.

"Why?" she asked, chewing on her bottom lip.

"Why what?" I asked, snapping back to reality.

"Why would you help someone like me? You probably have better stuff to do than waste your time on me."

My heart ached that she could possibly think she wasn't worth helping. I wanted to pull her into my arms and hold her until it erased all the hurt she'd been through, regardless of how inappropriate that may have seemed. Nobody should feel like they're a waste of time.

"You know I can't ever pay you back for" — she waved a hand indicating my place and the eaten meal — "all this. If I were to accept your offer. Hypothetically."

I already began shaking my head before she finished her sentence. "I wouldn't ever want you to pay me back." I thought about lying to her about why I wanted to help her but decided to go with the half-truth. "You looked sad. Your eyes. I want the chance to turn that around. However I can." I cleared my throat and looked away, rubbing my palms on the thighs of my jeans before getting up and gathering all our dirty dishes. I needed to do something to keep moving, or I was likely to scare her off. "The decision is solely up to you, though. If that's not where you're at right now, then no harm, no foul. There's a shower if you'd like to use it. We can part ways here."

"And if I don't?" She paused and took a deep breath before continuing. "Want to part ways?"

Something in my gut gave a little kick, but I ignored it and pushed it away. I focused on loading the rest of the dishes in the dishwasher before turning back to give her my full attention. She'd grabbed a paper towel and was wiping down the counter. "I'm heading up there tomorrow. You're welcome to stay here and then join me at the cabin."

Her hand paused in the circular motion, and her teeth sank into her bottom lip again. I could tell she was trying to supress another yawn, and was beginning to think it was a nervous habit. She answered with a subtle dip of her chin and resumed cleaning the counter. I watched her for a few more seconds before deciding that I was being a creep.

"I need to make a work call, but I'll leave an extra towel and toothbrush in the bathroom in case you'd like to shower and get comfortable."

I waited for a moment, but when she still hadn't responded, I pressed Start on the dishwasher and made my way to the master bedroom. I grabbed an extra pair of black sweatpants I hadn't worn in years and an old college shirt and thick socks from the dresser. I stopped at the linen closet in the hallway and grabbed an extra towel and face cloth, then placed all the items on the counter in the bathroom. I added an unopened toothbrush to the pile from the extras I usually kept under the sink for when any of my siblings got drunk in the city and stayed over instead of taxiing it back to their place.

When I passed back through the open living area to go onto the balcony, Leah was looking at my collection of movies. I internally groaned at what she saw. My siblings all made fun of my Disney and Pixar collection because what grown man collected animated movies? But I couldn't care less. They were a big part of our childhood. Plus, my sister's kids loved them when they came over to Uncle Deacon's house.

I chuckled as I closed the patio door behind me and

stepped up to the railing. My niece was turning into quite the Disney nerd herself.

I spent the next little while getting everything sorted for the job site for the next week. I had a feeling we'd be up at the cabin for a lot longer than that, but I could always delegate duties to someone else if needed. The joys of owning my company.

After I made sure orders were placed and the guys I employed knew what was to be done this week, I sent a quick text to my brother asking him what I should expect from someone going through withdrawal. Then I pocketed my phone and went back into the apartment. The quiet apartment. The absence of the sound of running water or the TV was loud.

"Leah?" I called, already knowing I wouldn't find her in the apartment.

I sighed and made my way to the kitchen. I had put the offer out there; that was all I could do.

A folded-up napkin on the counter caught my attention as I reached out to open the fridge. Abandoning the thought of getting something to drink, I picked it up and opened it.

I'm sorry. I can't
~ Leah.

Chapter Four

Leah

AS MUCH AS I WANTED TO TAKE DEACON UP ON HIS offer, I just… couldn't. I knew myself enough to know that I wasn't ready to embark on that journey. I wasn't ready for the ghosts of my past to make a reappearance, not after I spent so long trying to silence them. But as I returned to the area just outside of downtown Adelaide known to the locals as tent city, I knew I had made a mistake. One that could end up costing me my life.

I figured I hadn't used in over twenty-four hours and was itching for my next hit. I felt jittery, uneasy, like there was something crawling around under my skin, and no matter how much I scratched, I couldn't abate the itch. Plus, the voices had started getting louder. Telling me how much of a waste of space I was. Like I didn't already know that.

I stopped at the big blue tent kitty-corner to my small red one and called out to the owner. Pops poked his head out the opening. His grey hair was mussed like he hadn't brushed it in days, and living like we did, it wouldn't have surprised me if that were the case. He had a line indented across his face, most likely from the corded bracelet around his wrist and having fallen asleep on his arm. When he saw it was me, he gestured for me to follow him inside.

"Hey, Pops," I said as I ducked down under the opening and stepped inside his tent. I stayed at the entrance and minded my step. Pops was like the grandpa to everyone at tent city, hence the name. Nobody knew his real name, but everyone knew him as Pops. He took care of everyone; however, you could tell when he was struggling with his mental health because he shut down, and his tent became a land mine of dirty sharps, mouldy food, clothes, and pieces of random electronics. Today, his tent was particularly bad. "How's it going?" I asked, hoping today would be the day he decided to open up, but all I got in response was a grunt. "You got any down?"

He dropped down onto what I knew was a sleeping bag currently covered in a heap of clothes and other belongings and rummaged through a pants pocket before producing a baggy of the drug. I traded him the cash for the small Ziploc bag. I hesitated for a brief second and wondered if I should make a more solid effort to get him to talk, but I felt like I was going to crawl out of my skin if I didn't use in the next thirty seconds. I mumbled a thanks and left his tent, beelining it to my own. I hadn't been here in a couple of days, preferring to take my chance at trying to get in at the shelter for the last couple of nights than brave the cold here.

I breathed a relieved sigh and almost whooped in joy when I found a rig still in its packaging among my things. Unopened. The crippling fear that I may have had to wait longer to use was real.

That first hit… there's nothing like the euphoria that accompanies it. I swayed a little while sitting on my sleeping bag, and my eyes rolled back. Everything I had worried about or stressed over for the last couple of days just… vanished, and I was left in a cloud of nothingness.

It was great.

My breathing slowed as I relaxed back onto my pillow and let the drug take me wherever it wanted.

"Yo, Angel! Skeet and I are going to head over to 7-Eleven, you wanna come?" Maverick asked, his signature aviators in place over his eyes, as soon as I emerged from my tent several hours later. I hadn't planned on nodding out for that long, but I guessed I had taken a little more down than I thought I had.

"Yeah, count me in. I want a Slurpee," I answered, pulling the sweater up around my chin, ignoring the waft of male cologne as I joined the two men in front of Skeet's tent.

"Hey, you got a smoke?" Skeet asked.

I shook my head. "Sorry."

Maverick nudged his boyfriend in the shoulder playfully. "You know she doesn't smoke, man."

Nobody there knew how long they had been together or how long they'd been living out there for, but Skeet and Mav were the OG's of tent city. They were here before it was even coined tent city.

When I first made my way down there, they took me

under their wing and protected me. Called me their baby sis. I was grateful for their protection in my early days. If it weren't for them and Pops, I don't think I would've survived on the streets for as long as I had.

"Fuck, I forgot." He looked around until his gaze snagged on someone at the far end. "Hey, Douggie! You got a smoke?"

Douggie sat down on the trick bike he'd just swung his leg over and pulled out a pack of smokes from the inside pocket of his puffer jacket. Skeet whooped and dashed over to him. I grinned. You'd think he won the lottery or something with how excited he was.

"Alright, let's go," he said once he made his way back over to me and Mav, lit cigarette dangling from the corner of his lips like he was in some old-school fighter movie, blond hair draped over one eye.

Mav slung an arm over his shoulder, and together we made our way out of downtown and up to the only 7-Eleven in town. Adelaide wasn't what I would call a small town. Nobody knew anyone's business, and it was easy enough to go unnoticed, but it wasn't big-city living either. It was comfortable.

We walked the several blocks to the new development part of the city, pretending we didn't notice the way mothers hurried their kids across to the other side of the street when they saw us coming, how people avoided brushing shoulders with us as we passed, or when the cashier at the convenience store tracked our every move.

"Grape and Coke?" Mav asked, gently nudging my arm with his as he slid in beside me in front of the Slurpee machine.

"Hmm," I hummed, my eyes tracking over the different flavours on offer. "Think I'm going to go with cream soda and root beer."

He chuckled. "Switching it up?"

I grinned and reached out to grab the largest-sized cup. "Life's too short to always get the same flavour."

He nodded, a giant smile still plastered on his face. "Touché."

Mav chose the pop he wanted for his Big Gulp, and then the two of us joined Skeet up at the cash register, where he had already been waiting for us. The cashier still looked skeptical until we all produced enough money to pay for our drinks and Skeet's chocolate. It had been a particularly good month for bottles. It wasn't often that each of us was able to collect enough bottles for a Slurpee or, in Skeet and Mav's case, smokes, but when we did, the feeling was indescribable.

I was halfway to the door when I heard the cashier deny the purchase of a bottle of milk to the lady who had been standing behind us because she was short a dollar. She had a newborn baby strapped to her chest in one of those harness things and a toddler clinging to one of the pockets in her winter coat.

Without another thought, I rooted through all my pockets until I came up with just enough change and laid the coins on the counter.

"Thank you," she whispered, embarrassment coating her words. I smiled to let her know it was all good and then turned back to join my friends outside, ignoring the way the cashier narrowed his eyes in suspicion.

Mav shook his head when I joined them outside. "Why do you do that? She'd never do the same for any of us."

I shrugged and stabbed the ice in my drink with the purple straw. "Maybe, maybe not, but those kids don't know any different."

I huddled against the side of the building as Mav and

Skeet got out their pipes. Skeet offered me a hoot off his, but I shook my head. Smoking wasn't my thing, whether it was cigarettes or something harder.

As they did their thing, I let my mind wander back to Deacon. I wondered if he had made it to the cabin already, and if he had, then what was he doing right now? I folded my arms across my middle and leaned my head against the cold building as I thought about what it could've been like if I had accepted his offer of help. Just as soon as I thought it, I shook it off. Nothing good could come of it now. It was too late.

Once they were done their hoots and threw out their pipes, we started back to tent city again. We stopped along the way to get more harm reduction supplies. Just before we turned into the abandoned parking lot where tent city was located, Skeet turned around to face me and Mav and walked backwards. "You still good to come to the meet day after tomorrow?"

The day after tomorrow was Wednesday, the 16th, cheque day. Mav and I agreed to go with Skeet to meet with this new supplier he'd been vying to get in with for a hot minute.

Chapter Five

Deacon

It was another warm morning in Adelaide. Spring was well on the way. I woke up to the mid-March sun streaming brightly through the opening in the curtains that covered the windows of my bedroom.

I got out of bed and changed into a pair of running shorts before heading downstairs to throw together a protein smoothie. While the blender was on, I grabbed my phone and checked in with a few of my guys at different jobs sites all over town. The thing I had come to appreciate about being the owner of my company was that I didn't need to be on-site every day, not like when I first started the rock wall company.

Now, I had a handful of men I trusted to oversee the various sites whenever I took a much-needed day off, like today. But much like today, whenever I took the day off, I had to hit the gym so I could keep my strength up. It was more about preventing injuries than trying to lose weight.

I pocketed my phone just as the blender turned off and switched out the blade on the cup for a drinking lid before grabbing my gym bag from where I'd placed it by the door last night. I jogged down the three flights of stairs to the underground parking garage and jumped in my truck. I still couldn't believe that after years of working long hours, I was able to buy my dream truck in cash. No monthly payments. No interest. It was all mine. I grinned as I scrolled through the music app until I found my favourite workout playlist and hit shuffle. Today was going to be a good day. I could feel it.

JUST OVER AN HOUR LATER, I WAS DRENCHED IN SWEAT and breathing hard as I wiped down my workout station and headed for the shower. My mom would kill me if I showed up at Sunday family brunch a sweaty mess. Although, the thought of terrorizing my brothers with the stench was kind of appealing.

I quickly showered and changed into jeans and a pullover hoodie under my jacket before braving the wind. It may have seemed warm when I woke up this morning, but the sun was deceiving when the wind picked up.

Twenty minutes later, I pulled into the driveway of my childhood home and parked behind my brother's lifted truck. I rolled my eyes with a chuckle. This driveway sure looked different now that we all had our own vehicles. I loved that my parents had moved into this little house when they were first married and still decided to stay in it after Lilah, the youngest, got married three years ago and moved out.

My niece and nephew's laughter were the first sounds I heard as I opened the front door and stepped inside. The smell of bacon and french toast made my stomach growl as I inhaled deep and felt myself relax for the first time in days.

"Uncle Deacon!" The four-year-old twins squealed as they raced each other to see who could get to me first. They both crashed into my legs at the same time, and if I hadn't been prepared for the impact, I would've been pushed down by the sheer force.

I chuckled and ruffled a hand over their heads. "Hey, munchkins. What are you two up to?"

"Uncle Dash brought us rugby balls," my niece exclaimed, bouncing excitedly on her feet after she let go of my leg.

"But Mom and Grandma won't let us play with them in the house." My nephew pouted.

I had to bite my lip from laughing. That pout paired with the sparkle of mischief in his green eyes made him look exactly like his mother when she was his age. I had no doubt that by the end of brunch, there'd be a couple of broken picture frames and maybe a dent or two in the walls to match the ones already there. The ones that were put there by his mother.

"How about we go to the rec centre after we eat? Then you can ask Uncle Dash to show you how he makes it spin like he does on TV."

Their faces lit up instantly at the suggestion before they took off running in the direction of the kitchen, yelling for my brother. Dash had got an offer to play for the Canadian rugby team right out of college. It had always been his goal in life to play in the Rugby 7s and at the summer Olympics. His first goal came true three seasons ago and his second last summer. We were all incredibly proud of him and his dedication to the sport.

I followed my niece and nephew through the living room and down the hall to the kitchen, where everyone was already gathered. Or not everyone. As I scanned the faces sitting and standing around the counter, I noticed one of my brothers was missing.

"Hey, big bro," Lilah said before crunching down on a carrot and curling an arm around my waist. I pulled her into my chest and squeezed maybe a little harder than needed. I grinned when she started to squirm and pushed against my chest.

"You're so annoying," she groused when I finally let her go.

"But you love me." I tugged on the end of her ponytail like I used to do when we were kids. She rolled her eyes at the familiar gesture while the corner of her lips twitched up in a smile.

"Van not here?" I asked.

"No. Dad was on the phone with him when he got another call just before his shift was supposed to be over. He should be here soon," she added as she looked around at our other siblings.

Dash looked up from where he was showing our dad a video on an iPad and lifted his chin in greeting before going back to it.

Damien came over and silently handed me a beer. Ever since he left the army, he'd been quiet, only talking when spoken to directly or if he deemed something worthy of a conversation. I still worried about him being cooped up alone in his house out in the country and only surfacing for family brunch.

"You good?" I asked him after taking a drink.

He eyed me over the neck of his own bottle. His eyes weren't the same green as the rest of our siblings and our dad. Instead, they matched the honey colour of our mom's. He shrugged after several moments and took another drink. "Yeah," he said, his voice hoarse.

I decided to leave it at that, knowing it was the most I was going to get out of him today. I slapped him on the back and excused myself to go greet our mom, who was busy in the kitchen making pancakes, bacon, and eggs with our other brother.

The song on the radio changed. Drake took hold of one of Mom's hands and pulled her into him. His arm wrapped around her waist, his other hand clasping hers as he danced her around the kitchen. She threw her back and laughed, and the lines around her eyes deepened with the sound. The sun coming in through the kitchen window made her look like an angel.

I placed my beer bottle on the counter and cleared my throat. "May I cut in?" I asked when the two of them turned around.

They wore matching grins as Drake let go of her and bowed out. "I'll go set the table."

"Hi, Mom," I greeted her as I took her tiny frame in my arms and continued to dance her around the kitchen as a Michael Bolton song played through the cassette player on the counter beside the fridge.

"Hi, baby." She beamed. Her love for me was obvious in the shine in her eyes.

As kids, we used to watch our dad grab her around her waist while she cooked us dinner and dance with her around the kitchen, twirling her out and catching her again. It never failed to put a smile on her face. As we grew up, it felt natural that us kids would act as a stand-in from time to time. We'd even made Lilah join in by standing on our feet and dancing with her as another one of us danced with Mom. I guessed it became a kind of tradition. Out of all of us, Damien and I weren't the dancers, but regardless, I looked forward to the day when I could carry on the tradition with my wife.

As the song wound down to an end, I spun her out and then dipped her when she spun back into my arms. She laughed and playfully slapped my arm when I brought her back up again.

"Alright, enough of that. Van will be here soon, and then we can all eat," she said, shooing me out of her kitchen. When I caught my dad's eyes from across the room, he winked and then went back to watching whatever Dash was showing him. It must have been game footage if they were that invested.

Van showed up a little while later, apologizing for being late. We all crowded around the large dining table Dad had custom built around the time I turned sixteen. It was solid cherry wood, with intricately carved designs running up the sides. It had an extension that went in the middle for anytime Mom and Dad hosted Christmas dinner with a few extra guests or for when each of us brought someone home.

Brunch turned out great. I used to hate these weekly family get-togethers — maybe hate was too strong a word for what I felt — but now I started looking forward to them. Since Van and Lilah cleaned up last week, this week the duty fell to me and Drake. I turned the coffee maker on as Drake collected the plates. Once it was done, I took our parents a refill of their coffees and then got going on loading the dishwasher while Drake tackled washing the bigger dishes by hand.

"How's school going?" I asked my brother as I put

the last plate in the dishwasher, added a pod, and closed it.

Drake and Van were the middle siblings, with me and Damien being the oldest and Dash and Lilah being the youngest. Lilah was technically the baby at twenty-four, but don't let her hear someone say that. We'd learned long ago to never use her name and "baby" in the same sentence.

Drake blew out a frustrated breath, and for the first time, I noticed dark circles under his eyes. I wondered if he had been sleeping at all. He was the scholar out of all of us. He worked hard and always pushed himself in his academics. Sometimes too hard, to the point of forgetting to eat and not sleeping.

He placed the last pan in the drying rack and dried his hands before he turned around and leaned against the counter, resting his palms on the marble surface.

"Honestly? I'm rethinking if this whole doctor thing is for me."

That took me by surprise. Drake had always had dreams of becoming a doctor and working with youth who struggled with mental health and addiction. He wanted to treat the whole person, mind and body.

"Why do you think that?"

He dropped his head and studied the tile under his feet for several minutes. I left him to his thoughts in silence but maybe regretted that decision when he met my eyes again and had closed his walls.

"It's fine. I'll figure it out," he said as he pushed off the counter.

"You sure, man?" I wanted to push him to talk to me, but I knew my brother. If I kept insisting, he would close up more.

He nodded. "Yeah. Thanks, though."

I still wasn't fully convinced that everything was okay, but I could tell he was done with the conversation, so I let it go and followed him back out to the living room, where our other siblings had congregated to watch the game.

"It was crazy. I thought for sure we had lost her. It was a damn miracle that we were able to bring her back," Van was saying as Drake and I entered the room.

"Talking about your last call?" I asked and dropped down to sit on the long L-shaped couch beside him. I reached across him and grabbed a handful of the popcorn Dash had in a bowl in his lap. He grumbled about us all getting our own damn snacks, but we ignored him.

"Yeah. An OD out behind that new dollar store that just went up by you."

"Man, this new drug that's going around is something else. Narcan doesn't even work on it. It's crazy," Drake said from the other side of the couch.

Van nodded. "Right? I mean, it'll still kinda work if the drug is mostly mixed with fentanyl, which seems to be the case, but we never know when we get to a scene unless they were using with someone and the person still happened to be on-site. Shit, she looked young, though, like Lilah's age. Maybe a little older," he added after we were all quiet for a while. "She had some pretty neat ink along her collarbone too."

Dash chuckled. "You perving on your patients now, Van?"

"No, asshat." He clipped our brother on the back of the head. "We had to move the zipper of her sweater a bit so we could do chest compressions."

My brothers gave Dash a hard time for his comment, but I had lost track of the conversation. My brain was still on the fact that the woman who had OD'd blocks from my house had a tattoo in the same place Leah had. A fact I'd only noticed because her shirt was ripped from the men in the alley when I brought her home. Maybe it was just a coincidence, but I couldn't shake the uneasy feeling that settled in my gut.

"Wh —" I cleared my throat and tried to swallow past the lump that took residence. "What did she look like?"

Van gave me a weird look and opened his mouth — I assumed to call me a weirdo for wanting to know what his patient looked like — but he must have changed his mind once he got a look at my face because all humour left his.

"Hey, Deac, you okay, man? You look like you've seen a ghost," Drake commented, but I ignored him. My gaze was still focused on Van.

"She, uh, had long, dark brown hair. Dark brown eyes, too, with gold in them."

I was up and moving toward the front door before he finished talking. I ignored all the calls of my name and questions from my parents and sister as to where I was going. I grabbed my jacket from the hook and practically ran toward my truck. I prayed that Van's description really was just a coincidence and it wasn't Leah lying in a hospital bed right now because she'd OD'd. As much as the thought would make me an asshole, I fucking hoped that it was someone else.

Chapter Six

L^{eah}

I WAS POUTING LIKE A PETULANT CHILD, AND I KNEW IT. But I hated being poked and prodded while being looked down upon because my coping mechanism happened to be heroin instead of the more acceptable ones like wine or the gym. To each their own.

My reason for pouting wasn't because I had ended up in hospital this time; it was because I was glad that I had, and I didn't want to think too closely about the reason why. Even still, I felt restless. I couldn't stop moving my legs, shifting from side-to-side, and yawning. I needed to use and soon. I frowned and cursed myself out. No, I didn't. I'd made up my mind this time. Last night was the last time I picked up a rig.

Just as I had laid my head back against the uncomfortable bed in a curtained-off room in the emergency department and blew out a breath, footsteps pounded down the hallway and stopped right outside my door. My heart raced.

I had fervently hoped that he wouldn't show. Since I didn't have any next of kin listed, the nurses had asked if I wanted them to call the person whose name was on the dog tags in my pocket. I refused, but apparently, they had done it anyway. I didn't want him to see me like this or to have to face him again after I stole from him *after* he had been kind enough to offer me a safe place to spend the night. I groaned and squeezed my eyes shut. I was an asshole.

The screech of the curtain being pushed open made my head snap up. Our eyes met immediately, and it felt like I was drowning in a pool of dark green seafoam. A thunderstorm brewed in that gaze, and I swallowed thickly with it all directed at me. As soon as he took in all of me, though, the storm melted away on a relieved breath, but that couldn't be right.

"How are you doing?" The question took me by surprise, just like seeing him standing there did.

"Uh, okay. I guess?" *Lie.* I wouldn't be okay for a long time. Not as long as I was still dependant on heroin.

He came further into the room and took my hand in his while he plonked down in the chair beside the hospital bed. I didn't flinch at the touch that time. I stared at him for what felt like hours as I tried to work out why in the hell he was here, aside from being told that some random had his dog tags on her when she was brought into the hospital from a suspected overdose.

When he didn't attempt to explain himself either, I decided that I couldn't take the suspense anymore. I had to distract myself from the soothing motion of his thumb rubbing over my knuckles. It had been a while since anybody had touched me with such gentleness.

"What are you doing here?"

"My brother told me you had been brought in?"

I froze. "What?"

"Okay, not really. But he said he was late getting to brunch because he had a call about a suspected overdose close to my apartment, and when I asked him about it, he described you. I wanted to make sure you were okay."

I smiled despite myself. He looked nervous. Like maybe he thought I would find fault in him wanting to make sure I was okay. After all, I'd only met the guy once.

His rambling was cute.

"So, you're not here because of the dog tags?"

His thumb stopped on its upward stroke, and he cocked his side as he searched my eyes. A slow, knowing smile spread across his handsome face. "No, I'm not here because of the dog tags."

I sucked in a breath. "You knew." It wasn't a question.

His smile grew. "I noticed they were gone around the same time I noticed that you were too."

I slumped back against the bed. "Oh."

"Hey." He gently squeezed my hand to get my attention. "It's okay. Obviously you needed them more than I did."

I studied the man beside me. How could he possibly be that understanding? I took something that belonged to him. As far as he knew, I'd probably pawned it for cash for more drugs. Yet, there was no look of disgust or anger at having something important to him being taken. There was just understanding. Something I didn't deserve. I squirmed under his watchful gaze.

I didn't know how to process any of this.

"Want to talk about it?" he asked.

I flinched, having momentarily forgotten why I was in there. "I trusted the wrong people," I said and quickly looked away.

Truth be told, it wasn't the first time I had overdosed, but it was the first time I had been left alone. That part hurt the most. If some random dollar store customer hadn't found me and called 911…

I shivered thinking about what could have happened. I never wanted to experience that again. I debated on asking him if the offer of his cabin was still on the table, but guilt gnawed at me over having left him without an explanation a few days ago.

"What is it?"

I lifted my gaze to his face at his question and bit my lip.

"What were you wanting to ask?"

"It's nothing," I replied.

"Tell me. Please, Leah."

My belly tightened and swooped at hearing my name on his lips. I took a deep breath and let the question out in a rush as I exhaled, half praying he wouldn't be able to make out the words and we'd just change the subject.

"Isyourcabinstillavailable?"

"I thought you weren't ready?" he said after several excruciating seconds. He'd been referring to the cop-out note I left for him.

"Yeah, well…" I shrugged. "This time around, almost dying kinda changed my mind about the whole thing."

I hadn't meant to come out sounding so nonchalant about it, but that thunderous expression was back on Deacon's face. I felt like shit.

"Is that what you do? Make jokes about overdosing?"

Even as he gritted his teeth and anger rolled off him in waves, he never removed his hand from mine or tightened his grip. That alone said more about his character than any words he spoke the last time we met.

"No. I..." I slipped my hand out from under his so that I could sit up in the bed and then tentatively placed it on top of his again. For some reason, I needed his touch. "It's a defensive mechanism. When I'm anxious or nervous, I make a joke about the situation or laugh. I know it's messed up, but..." I trailed off and lowered my gaze. "I'm sorry," I whispered.

He blew out a rushed breath and ran a hand through his hair. I didn't know why it had taken me so long to notice he was wearing glasses. He hadn't been wearing them the last time I saw him. The clear, slightly oversized frames looked good on him. They kind of gave him the sexy, older professor vibes. I bit my bottom lip as a blush worked its way across my cheeks.

"Yes."

The one word took me by surprise. After his outburst, I was sure he would have said no to helping me out. I wasn't sure if the 'yes' was to my question about his cabin or to something else.

"Yes, the cabin's still available," he repeated. "I never ended up going there the other day, so we'd have to stop for supplies on the way up."

Warmth bloomed inside me, but I was still hesitant to get my hopes up. What if this didn't work? What if I couldn't do it?

I chewed on my lip as I thought about the tent that had been my home for the last several years. It had become like a security blanket of sorts. I knew what to expect there. I knew the dangers and how to navigate or avoid them. How to survive. The world outside of tent city was big, and I was scared that maybe it would be a little overwhelming too.

"How are you feeling right now?" Deacon asked. I tilted my head, considering his question. "Are you…" He stopped, like he was considering whether he should continue with his question or not. "Are you wanting to use right now?"

"I always want to use," I answered honestly and without hesitation. "I don't think that craving ever truly goes away. But yes. Because they had to Narcan me, it reversed the effects of the drugs, so the urge to use is even higher now." I knew it probably wasn't what he wanted to hear, but it was the truth.

He didn't get a chance to respond when the curtain pulled open again and the emergency department doctor walked in. From the corner of my eye, I saw Deacon pull out his phone and type out a message to someone. I half listened to the doctor as he told me what I already knew and offered to get me into treatment. I nodded along to whatever was said until that point but politely declined his offer and told him I'd be fine. With a reserved sigh that said he'd heard that before, he told me I was free to go.

Deacon helped me off the bed, and I smiled in thanks as I slipped my feet back into my worn boots. I didn't have a coat on me when they brought me in, so there wasn't anything else to collect around the room before we could go.

Once the warm March air hit my face, I relaxed for the first time since the ambulance arrived at the hospital. I hated that place. Hated the smell. Most of all, I hated the memories being in there tried to resurface.

"Are you hungry? We could eat now or after we get

groceries," Deacon asked once we were settled in his truck.

"I could eat," I lied.

Truthfully, I wasn't all that hungry, but I needed something to take my mind off the clawing need that was trying to rip a hole through me, and I needed it soon or I was going to try and score again.

Deacon pulled into a drive-thru and ordered a couple of burgers and fries for both of us as well as a couple of coffees. I vowed to myself that as soon as I could, I would pay him back for everything he'd done for me.

We stopped at the grocery store next, and I felt like a lost puppy while I followed him around the store, but I also kind of liked it. I'd never gone grocery shopping with anyone before.

After I got over the initial awkwardness when he'd asked me what I liked and I would shrug, I relaxed. There were several times it got overwhelming with all the choices — seriously, why were there so many options for the same thing? — but Deacon would casually choose two or three and put them in the cart. I told him it was all too much — surely two people didn't need three types of cheese or cereal.

As we got into the checkout line, Deacon's phone pinged again. It had been going off sporadically while we were in the store, but he didn't do more than glance at it. This time, he typed out a quick message, then helped me unload the items from the cart into the truck.

It wasn't until we'd packed the grocery bags into the cab of the truck and were on the road again that he spoke.

"I had my sister grab a couple of items of clothes for you. They're in the bag in the back."

I'd noticed the bags when we were loading the groceries but figured I'd missed seeing them earlier. I hadn't even thought about clothes. I looked down at the worn jeans and sweater and couldn't remember the last time I had changed. A lead weight settled in my stomach. I wondered not for the first time why a man like Deacon would ever offer me help.

"Thank you." I looked over my shoulder but only noticed one duffle bag half-buried under plastic bags. "What about you?"

"I always keep a couple changes of clothes at the cabin," he replied, switching lanes.

I raised an eyebrow in a silent bid for him to explain. He glanced at me before returning his attention back to the road and chuckled.

"Some trips up there are spontaneous. Maybe more so than my family would like."

"They don't like you going up there?"

"It's not that they don't. But there are no cell towers within range. No way of communicating with the outside world. My parents like all of us to check in periodically so that they know we're okay. It's a habit they established when Damien and I enlisted. We checked in whenever we could, but sometimes it would be months before we were able to."

"What about your cat?"

"My sister and one of my brothers will check in on Lumière occasionally."

I grinned but bit back any comment on him naming his cat after a Disney character. I couldn't deny that it was cute, though. Something else he said intrigued me too.

"How long were you enlisted?"

"About eight years. Damien received a medical

discharge about seven years into our enlistment. Before we signed up, we made a pact that we would always serve together. When one of us wanted out, we both got out. After he was sent home, I finished my remaining time and got out."

"Damien? Your brother?"

"Yeah. Not the one who brought you in. That's Van."

"How many siblings do you have?" I asked, mildly shocked.

"There's six of us in total. Damien, Donovan, Dash, Drake, and Delilah's the baby. But don't tell her I said that. She's likely to skin me alive if she knew I called her the baby of the group."

"That must have been crazy growing up," I said and settled more comfortably into the seat.

"It was hectic. Five boys running around and a baby. My parents seemed to love it. According to them, they always wanted a full house." He glanced at me before turning his attention back to the road. "What about you? Any family?"

I sighed and brought my foot up on the seat. "Nah. Never knew my mom, and my dad died when I was three." I swallowed hard and blinked back the memory of that time while staring unseeingly through the window.

"I'm sorry. I didn't mean to —"

"It's not your fault," I cut him off before he could finish. "I was the one who brought up family."

We drove in silence for the rest of the way to the cabin.

Chapter Seven

D eacon

I FELT LIKE THE WORLD'S BIGGEST ASSHOLE. I COULDN'T have known that asking about her family would bring up painful memories, but obviously they had if the way she was huddled against the passenger door and staring intensely out the window had been any indication.

I concentrated back on the road, keeping an eye on the muddy edges of the mountain road. The last thing I wanted was for the edges to give way after being softened by all the melting snow. As I drove, I tried to search my brain for something to say that wasn't another apology. I knew she wouldn't appreciate that.

After several more minutes of navigating the switchback roads, the dense tree coverage opened to a small clearing. I breathed a sigh of relief at the first view of the cabin nestled at the back of the lot.

This, right here, was my sanctuary. My home away from home. My escape.

I hoped it would do for Leah what this place did for me after I left the army.

Leah

My jaw dropped as Deacon pulled the truck to a stop outside the small mountain cabin. Snow still blanketed the ground up here, but it just added to the beauty of the place. A real winter wonderland. I hopped out of the truck and gravitated toward the frozen lake I could see past the cabin like I was in a trance.

Just beyond the porch that wrapped all the way around the back side of the house, the water was just starting to thaw out from being frozen all winter. I could easily picture long summer days spent swimming and fishing here. It was like someone plucked the perfect getaway out of my dreams and plopped it right here. It was unreal.

"This is… wow," I said when I heard Deacon walk up behind me.

"Welcome to my home away from home," he said.

We continued to admire the view before us for several more minutes before I heard the crunch of Deacon's boots in the snow as he turned back to start unloading the truck and then unlocked the front door. I let my gaze sweep over everything one more time before I joined him and grabbed several bags of groceries.

He pushed open the front door and kicked off his shoes. The cabin wasn't any bigger than his place back in the city. It was nice. Cozy. A fireplace took up most of the main wall across from a love seat framed by two bookshelves. It looked like the perfect place to cuddle up with a mug of tea and either a good show or a book. I didn't think I'd be getting much time for that, though. Not with the hurdles I had in front of me.

"Bedroom is through that door. Bathroom is over there and kitchen and living room, obviously." He grinned and turned in a circle, pointing out the respective doors.

"Only one room?" I asked.

"I'll take the couch. You're in for a few hard days. You're going to need all the comfort you can get for a while," he replied like he could read my thoughts.

"I don't want to put you out any more than I already have."

"Leah, it's fine. I knew what I was getting into when I offered this to you. Plus, the couch isn't half-bad."

He looked stricken, like he somehow made a mistake he wasn't aware of. "I'm sorry. Do you not want me to call you that? Is there something else you want to be called?"

I smiled and placed a hand on his arm to gain his attention. "You're fine. People on the streets called me Angel." I paused, shook my head, then continued. "Please call me Leah. Angel is… part of my past now."

"Because you look so innocent?"

I cocked my head at the question.

Then he clarified, "The name?"

There was no malice behind his words. My lips twitched into a smile. I was far from innocent. Everyone knew that. I was sure even he knew that.

"Because I have an angelfish tattoo on my shoulder."

Even though he couldn't see it, I still reached over with my opposite hand and pointed to the spot.

There were times I could still feel the vibration and the hours spent in the chair. Back when the pain of a new tattoo was enough to dull the sting of my past.

"You like marine animals?" he asked while unpacking the plastic bags.

"Love them." I bit my lip as I tried to think about how to bring something up. "Hey, uh…" I paused and debated if I wanted to do this. If I did, there really was no going back. I was in this. I knew Deacon wouldn't go back on his word if he promised me what I was about to ask. "If I ask you to take me back, promise me you'll listen."

He paused putting the groceries away and studied me for a minute. I tried not to squirm under all that attention, but it was useless, so I grabbed some of the groceries and started opening drawers and cabinets until I found where they went.

A hand landed on my shoulder. I turned to face him. His eyes had softened into understanding and not the pity I half expected.

"I promise."

He tucked a strand of hair that had fallen loose from my ponytail behind my ear, and I smiled as a blush crept its way across my cheeks.

"I'm going to go make sure we have enough firewood for tonight, then I'll get dinner started. Make yourself at home," Deacon said and pulled away. He went about collecting the empty grocery bags and headed back out the front door.

I felt a sense of relief that he had agreed to my request. I hoped he meant it because I had no doubt that as my withdrawal got worse over the coming days, I'd do anything for him to take me back to town so that I could get high. I needed to know that he would be strong enough for the both of us.

Deacon

She looked so small standing in the doorway. Like a baby deer ready to bolt at the first sign of danger. It was all I could do not to take her in my arms and hold her until the tension in those shoulders eased. I had no idea what her life story was, but I had this insane urge to fight all of her demons. There was a sadness in her eyes — something I had noticed that very first day — that made me want to do whatever I could to make her smile and laugh. I told myself that was why I was doing this. Why I had offered up my cabin when I usually preferred not to have any company. I'd have done it for anyone. But the way she had blushed under my touch had given me inappropriate thoughts too. I fought them back. She wasn't much older than my sister. I just had to keep thinking of her that way.

I had noticed the firewood pile had been a little lacking when we brought the bags in, so I went around the side of the cabin and let my mind go blank as I chopped more logs to add to the pile. I wasn't sure how long we were going to stay up here or if there was any snow more in the forecast, so I chopped until my arms were burning and sweat ran down my face and back.

By the time I headed back to the cabin, I was looking forward to a hot shower. I pushed open the pinewood door and came to an abrupt stop. I wasn't sure what I had expected to find when I went inside, but what I saw was not it. Leah paced nervously around the length of the large open space; her hair had come undone from the high ponytail she'd had it in earlier when we left the hospital. It looked like she had been tugging on the brown strands the entire time I'd been gone. Her eyes were wild as they darted around the room, and she chewed on her thumb.

"Hey, is everything okay?" I asked, keeping my voice low so as not to startle her, but the attempt was in vain as she jumped anyway at the sound of my voice.

She shook her head hard. "No. I can't. I can't do this."

My brows drew down in confusion until she dropped her arms and started scratching at her skin. I had wondered how long it would take before she'd start going through withdrawal. When we first arrived at the cabin, I had texted Drake and asked him what signs to look out for and what to do.

"What the fuck, man?" he asked when my phone rang as I stood watching Leah take in the river and everything else around the cabin.

"I don't have time to explain right now. Just tell me what to do."

He sighed. "Alright, but you're going to explain the next time I see you," he said, and I reluctantly agreed, knowing that my brother wouldn't let up until I gave in.

I hastily toed off my boots and went to her. I was worried if I didn't distract her soon, she wouldn't stop scratching until she hurt herself. So, I took her hands in mine and dipped down until I caught her eyes.

"Yes, you can. You can do this."

She kept shaking her head. "No. No, I'm sorry. I can't." Her face crumpled, and she pitched forward into my chest. "Make it stop." She sniffed. "Please, I'll do anything. Please, take me into town, and I can use just a little bit. It'll be fine. I promise. Please," she begged, and I felt my heart crack at the pain in her eyes.

"I'm sorry, Leah, but no." I had made a promise to her, after all. If I hadn't promised her, I don't know if I would have given in to her pleas. Seeing her so broken nearly undid me.

"It hurts. It hurts so much," she sobbed. I let go of her hands, and she clutched the back of my jacket.

I smoothed a hand down the back of her head as I tried to soothe her. Her tears soaked into the front of my shirt, but I didn't care. I would hold her like this the entire time we were here if it helped her even a fraction.

Eventually, she allowed me to move us over to the couch. I sat with her head in my lap and continued to stroke her hair and down her arm until she fell asleep.

Chapter Eight

L eah

"Daddy," I called, poking my head out of the bedroom to see if I could see him in the living room at the end of the hallway. I knew he'd told me to stay in my room until he came to get me, but my tummy was starting to hurt. "Daddy," I called again, clutching my favourite blanket closer as I pulled the door open wider. I waited and listened for him to call me out, but it was quiet.

I slowly walked down the hallway, afraid that he would be mad if he saw me come out of my room too soon. I couldn't find Daddy. I picked up my stool and moved it in front of the cereal. I put my blanket on the floor, then stepped on the stool so I could reach my favourite cereal. I smiled when I got the box and stepped down. After I poured it into a pink bowl, I picked up my blanket and went to sit on the couch to watch cartoons. Daddy was sleeping on the floor.

"Silly Daddy," I said.
He never woke up.

I jolted awake, tangled in forest-green sheets that were soaked through with my sweat. It had been years since I'd dreamt about my dad. I groaned as I tried to roll over, but the sudden nausea made me stop. It felt like the room was spinning, and I had no choice but to try and hold on for dear life. I had heard stories from people at tent city about their experience with withdrawal, but I never gave any thought to how bad it would feel. If this was how the next several days were going to play out, then I was out. I couldn't do it. Pain laced my body, and that coupled with the nausea and dizziness made me feel like I was dying.

I was such an idiot. What made me believe I could possibly do this? Despite the sweat pouring from my body, or maybe because of it, I shivered violently and reached for the duvet to try and pull it over me. I squeezed my eyes shut under the covers and tried to push away the memories the dream dragged up. Nothing good ever came from revisiting my past.

The bedroom door opened, and I groaned at how loud it sounded in the otherwise quiet of the cabin.

"I brought you something to eat," Deacon said as the bed dipped.

I ignored him. It was his fault that I was in this stupid predicament in the first place. If he had only let me go to the nearest town, I wouldn't be in this pain. I wouldn't be starting to remember everything again.

"C'mon, Leah, you need to eat something."

I flinched away from his touch when a hand landed on my shoulder on top of the blanket. I could feel him hesitate and pull his hand back. I wasn't going to apologize. Not when I hated him for doing this to me.

"At least drink some orange juice. You need to stay hydrated."

After several minutes passed of me ignoring him, Deacon sighed and stood up. I heard what sounded like a glass being put down on the nightstand, and then footsteps retreated back towards the door.

"I've left towels and an extra toothbrush out in the bathroom. I'll check on you in a little bit again."

I tried to get more sleep after Deacon left, but I couldn't stay still long enough to let my body relax. I threw the covers back and got out of bed but remained in the room. I wouldn't be going out there. I'd stay in here until he agreed to take me into town. This was ridiculous anyway. I was a grown-ass woman. I could make my own damn decisions, and if I said that I changed my mind and couldn't do this, then I damn well knew what I was talking about.

I wandered over to the big window that overlooked a small clearing on the left side of the cabin. Deacon was out there. He didn't have his winter jacket on, instead opting for a red-and-black plaid button-up shirt and a black toque. He had his glasses on today, which usually clashed with the lumberjack look but on him looked good. Really good. I shook off that thought immediately and pushed away from the window. I didn't care what he was doing, but since I knew he was outside, I pulled open the bedroom door and ventured out into the open living space, making a dash for the front door. I barely stopped to get my feet into the shoes I had kicked off when we first got here. I swiped the truck keys from the thing on the wall and took off.

I ran across the porch and down the steps, just about making it to the truck. I had a hand on the handle when strong arms wrapped around my waist and lifted me up, carrying me back toward the cabin.

"No! Let me go." I kicked and wildly flailed my arms.

"Leah, stop." Deacon grunted as my elbow connected to his ribs. "Dammit, how are you so fucking strong." He didn't let me down until we were safely back inside the cabin and the door was closed. Even then, he put himself between me and the front door.

"You can't keep me here! It's kidnapping!"

He crossed his arms and raised an eyebrow. "I made you a promise. You can do this, Leah. Just a couple more days." His soft voice belied the tension and stone-like posture of his body. How could he be so fucking calm right now?

I was losing my mind, but I knew that even if I tried, there would be no getting through him unless I was ready to cause bodily harm, and even though I was hurting for another hit, I didn't want to hurt him. I wasn't that desperate yet.

"I can't, Deacon. It's too hard," I said as I shivered and wrapped my arms around my body. Pain gripped my stomach.

He dropped his arms and loosened his stance, taking a couple of steps toward me before he pulled me into his arms. I closed my eyes and pressed my cheek into his chest.

"You can. I'm right here with you. We'll get through this." His chest rumbled as he spoke the words. I wanted to believe him, but I knew it wasn't going to be as easy as he made it sound. "The soup should almost be done by now. How about we eat and watch a movie on the couch?"

I reluctantly let him go and sniffed, embarrassed by my outburst and escape attempt. "Yeah, okay."

Deacon went into the kitchen to check on the soup in the slow cooker. I sat on the couch and chewed the shit out of my thumbnail while I watched him move about the kitchen. He had so much faith in me that I was afraid I wouldn't be able to measure up to his expectations. People had looked up to me in the past, and I had let them down. That's what I did. I was a failure. Good for nothing.

You're such a waste of space, Leah.
We should've never given you a chance.
What'd we expect from a junkie whore.
No wonder her mother didn't want her.

The nausea came on fast and swift. I bolted for the bathroom and made it to the toilet in the nick of time.

For the life of me, I couldn't figure out why he was even helping me? I would just end up disappointing him and wasting his time. It was only a matter of time before he realized his mistake, and then he would kick me out, and I'd be right back downtown.

My thoughts continued on this downward spiral as I got sick while Deacon got our lunch together in the kitchen. I flushed the toilet and wiped my mouth before washing my hands. Hopefully he hadn't heard that.

I muttered a *thank you* and accepted the offered bowl as I sat back down on the couch, even as I tried to fight the self-deprecating thoughts that continued their onslaught.

I pushed the spoon through the liquid, lost in my own head. I had no appetite anyway but couldn't exactly say no when he offered to dish us up lunch. It smelled good, though, and my stomach growled regardless.

A weight settled on my chest, making bile start to rise

up the back of my throat again. No matter how much I swallowed, I couldn't stop the feeling of needing to throw up a second time. I practically threw the bowl onto the coffee table and ran to the bathroom, barely making it to the toilet before whatever was left in my stomach made a repeat appearance.

After I was sure that I couldn't possibly throw up more, I reached a shaking hand up to flush it, then dropped back down on my ass and leaned my head against the wall with a groan. I shivered and pulled my legs up, hugging them to my chest.

"Leah?" Deacon's voice sounded through the door, proceeded by a knock.

I tried to tell him to not come in here. I didn't want him to see me like this — I didn't want anyone to see me like this — but I couldn't get the words past my chattering teeth.

The door was pushed open the rest of the way. Deacon stepped through.

I groaned. "Just kill me."

"No can do," he said, bending to wrap his arms around me and stood me up. "Let's get you back to bed." He hooked one arm under my knees, the other under my arms and lifted me up, carrying me back to the bedroom.

"Don't go." I reached out to grab his arm once he'd gotten me settled back in the king-sized bed and made a move to leave. "Can… can you hold me for a bit?" Heat crept up my cheeks at the embarrassment I felt at having asked such a question of someone I didn't know very well.

Deacon's lips parted like he was going to say something but then closed them. I knew enough to know when someone was trying to come up with an excuse as to why they couldn't do something. I wasn't about to force him to cuddle with me. I let his arm go and turned on my side, facing the wall, and curled into a fetal position.

Several seconds went by, and I was sure he had left. But then the bed dipped, and strong arms maneuvered me until I was on my other side and tucked into his body. I squeezed my eyes shut as they burned with unshed tears. Human touch had been foreign to me for so long that I'd stopped craving it. Or it was more like I did everything to convince myself that I didn't need it.

But right now, in this moment, I needed it like I needed to not be in this much pain again. Like I needed another hit of heroin. After only being in his arms for less than a minute, I already knew that Deacon's touch was going to be my next addiction. One that had the potential to be so much worse than my drug of choice.

"T-Tell me som-something," I stuttered, burrowing further into his heat.

I hoped the shivering would stop soon because the force with which my body was shaking was starting to hurt.

"What do you want to know?" he asked as his fingers skimmed up and down my arm.

"An-anything."

Truthfully, he could've read the terms of service from any number of things, and I would've been okay with it. I just needed something to take my mind away from focusing on the pain. And his voice was surprisingly soothing.

"Sometimes I wish Damien and I never enlisted." His fingers stopped their caressing for several breaths and then started again. "I've never told anybody that."

"Why?"

"Why haven't I told anybody or —"

"Why do you wish you never enlisted?"

He blew out a breath, and my head raised and lowered with the expanse of his chest. "It's not that I regret serving my country. I hate what it did to my brother. Damien was... Before we enlisted, he was the class clown. The comedian of the family. Always laughing. Always quick to smile. That never changed when we first enlisted. But he wasn't the same when he came home. It's like the thing that made Damien who he was his entire life just... disappeared."

"What happened to him?"

"No one knows. We weren't in the same unit, and he refused to talk about it. I should've been there with him, though. He's my older brother, but I promised our mom we'd look out for each other. Have each other's backs."

I lifted my head from his chest and looked down at him, the pain my body was in momentarily forgotten as I stared into green eyes that had darkened with guilt.

"It wasn't your fault, Deacon. I've only known you a short time, but even I could tell that if you could have been there for him, you would've been."

Deacon grunted something in a non-answer. I laid my head back down and slid my arm around his waist. I knew my words probably meant nothing to him. I didn't know him enough to have that kind of effect, but I hoped he believed them all the same.

"Do you want to watch something, or are you tired?" he asked after a while.

I shifted my legs around a bit, feeling restless again. "I don't think I could sleep even if I wanted to." My body was drained from everything I had been putting it through, but my mind raced.

His body shifted beneath my cheek as he reached

over to the nightstand for the remote and shifted back. The TV mounted to the opposite wall flickered on, and I squinted against harsh, bright light until my eyes adjusted.

"Any preference?"

I shook my head as best I could in my position. "I haven't watched TV in years. Why don't you put on your favourite movie?"

There was an unusually long pause, and nothing moved on the screen. I lifted my head up again to see what the holdup was and found him staring at me, a peculiar look on his face.

"What?" I breathed out a laugh.

"I'm trying to figure out what you meant."

"Your favourite movie," I said again.

Deacon blinked at me. "Like, action? Comedy? Fantasy? Animated?"

Understanding dawned, and I grinned. "You don't have an overall favourite? Like one that stands above the rest?"

"You mean an overall favourite in one genre?"

The confused look that crossed his face was too cute. If I hadn't been feeling like shit, I probably would've messed with him some more. I snuggled back into his chest and said, "Surprise me."

Surprise me he did. A few seconds later, the Disney castle and logo appeared on the screen. I wondered if there would be a time when this man didn't take me by surprise.

Chapter Nine

D^{eacon}

THE NEXT FOUR DAYS PASSED BY IN RELATIVELY THE SAME way. Leah refused to sleep, staying up for a full twenty-four hours before her body had had enough and forced her to rest. Those days were the worst. She would wake up screaming and drenched in sweat. Her wild eyes would ping-pong around the room as if she had to reassure herself that she wasn't wherever her mind took her. There was one day she'd made me lock her in the bedroom because she was afraid of what she'd do if she didn't. I hated seeing her struggle like that. Again, I wished I could take on some of what she was feeling, even if only to make it a little easier for her.

However, the night we watched my favourite Disney movie was the one and only night she fell asleep in my

> sharing pain is the deepest act of love

arms. It was also the only one where she got a decent three hours of sleep straight with no nightmares or fever.

It took everything for me not to pull her into my arms again the next night, but I didn't bring her up here for that. After that first night, I knew I would have to keep my distance. Something happened whenever I was around her, and it was more than just feeling protective over her. I couldn't explain it, but I wanted to be around her constantly. Wanted to hold her hand and push her hair back when it fell in her face. I wanted to do things to her that definitely weren't appropriate seeing as how we weren't in a relationship. We weren't anything to each other. Maybe in another time and place, but this was not the time. Not when she was in the middle of detoxing.

When she woke up screaming like someone was trying to murder her, all of that resolve nearly went out the window. I startled awake and tumbled off the couch, my legs having gotten caught in the blanket. I hadn't known what had woken me at first, but then she screamed again, and I bolted toward the bedroom. Leah was thrashing about on the bed, her legs kicking at something that wasn't there, but her arms weren't moving. It was like they were being pinned down. I rushed to her side and tried to call her name, but it was no use — she couldn't hear me.

I took a chance and crawled onto the bed beside her. I gently lifted her and cradled her against me. Her whimpers and pleas asking the person in her dreams to stop nearly undid me. I called her name again, hoping that it combined with rocking her back and forth would pull her from whatever nightmare she was facing, but it didn't work.

I remembered when we were kids, my mom would sing us this song when we had nightmares that would instantly calm us down enough to sleep again. I frantically searched my brain for the lyrics and then prayed that it would help Leah.

Chapter Ten

L eah

SOMEONE WAS SINGING. I COULDN'T SEE WHO, BUT THE deep tenor of it sounded familiar. The figure that had pinned me down slowly eased its grip and then disappeared as the song continued. I looked around in the dark and tried to find where it was coming from, but it sounded as if it surrounded me. I was tired — so tired — and the voice offered comfort in rest and promised that things would look better in the light of a new dawn.

Four days passed of not being able to sleep until my body literally shut down and forced me to rest. When I was awake, it was a constant battle between body aches and shivers and trying to stop my mind from taking a deep dive off a cliff.

Without the drugs, I could no longer go on ignoring the hurts of my past. I knew that sooner or later I would have to confront them, or the need to use would grow bigger until I couldn't go another minute without using. I just hoped that I could put that day off for as long as I could because I knew it wasn't going to be pretty, and I didn't want to be around Deacon when shit the fan and my demons came out. If he didn't already think the worst of me, he certainly would once he learned about my past and the reason why I'd ended up on the streets.

The man deserved a fucking medal, though. Four days of putting up with my moody, bitchy ass. It was like I'd reverted back to being a hormonal teenager with mood swings. I yelled, laughed, cried, and threw things in between bouts of getting sick and wishing I would just die already.

It wasn't until the third day that I found out that Deacon would sing to me whenever I had nightmares or bouts of hallucinations. It was his voice I'd heard in my dream that night. I would never admit this to anyone, but his voice gave me comfort. It eased the turbulent storm inside me. It didn't completely take it away but made it bearable.

On the fifth day, I felt better than I had in a very long time. Lighter. Deacon was outside chopping more firewood, so I decided to make us dinner since he had been doing all the cooking from the minute we'd arrived at the cabin. I still remembered one of my dad's favourite recipes, and upon a curious inspection of the pantry and fridge, I knew we had all the required ingredients. I pulled out a couple of chicken breasts, sour cream, and parmesan cheese from the fridge and placed them on the counter before I headed for the pantry and pulled out all the spices I'd need and something for a side dish.

I was just putting the chicken in the oven when the front door opened, and Deacon came back inside. The days had gotten increasingly warmer while we'd been up here, but the evenings and nights were still pretty chilly. I wondered if the navy blue, long-sleeved Henley was enough to protect him against the elements.

Although, I wasn't complaining. It stretched nicely across his shoulders and biceps and pulled just tight enough against his chest that I thought I saw piercings in his nipples. I couldn't know for sure unless I wanted to risk being found staring. The light-wash jeans he wore fit in all the right places and made it hard not to be envious of his round… assets. I finally understood what people meant when they said they wanted to take a bite out of someone's ass because *fucking wow*.

"Smells good in here," Deacon commented, coming into the kitchen and rubbing his hands together.

I laughed. "It hasn't been in the oven long enough to smell of anything." I scooted past him to fill a pot with water and placed it on the stove. My body was still weak from the last several days, but I could at least do this for him.

When I looked back over my shoulder at Deacon, his cheeks were red. Whether it was from embarrassment at his comment or from the wind outside, I didn't know.

"I, uh, was talking about the candle." His gaze darted to the candle I had forgotten I'd lit prior to starting dinner. I'd found it on one of the bookshelves earlier, and when I lifted the lid, the scent had made me think of comfort.

"Oh," I said, feeling incredibly stupid.

"Hey." Deacon reached out and grabbed my hand, giving it a quick squeeze. "It's okay. You've had a rough few days."

I saw his lips moving, knew there were words coming out, but my entire focus was on my hand in his. The connection didn't last long. As soon as he realized that he still held my hand, he immediately let go and took a step away, a sheepish look on his face. I wanted to protest the move and take his hand back. Instead, I opened the pantry and grabbed a packet of rice, then turned my back on him.

"I'm going to go get cleaned up and check in with my brother."

I nodded, my back still to him. "Sounds good. I'll let you know when dinner's ready."

While Deacon was taking a shower and talking to his brother, the quiet in the main living space was too much for me to handle. He had a CD player set up in the far corner of the counter between the stove and the fridge. I turned it on and then hit Play, not really caring which CD was already loaded. I was still pleasantly surprised when Tom Jones's voice crooned through the speakers, and I couldn't stop the smile that pulled at my lips even if I tried.

I felt lighter as I moved about the kitchen, finishing the rice and gathering the plates and cutlery we'd be using. I wasn't aware that I was singing along with the words until Deacon came out of the bedroom. My jaw dropped as I took in his exposed chest. He didn't have the six-pack of abs that most women drooled over, but I didn't care. Deacon's body was made for cuddling, and I found myself missing the feel of his arms banded around me as I slept. I recovered quickly from my gawking as he pulled a white T-shirt over his head and effectively covered up his body, but not before I caught a glimpse of a small tattoo on his hip bone.

"What are you up to out here?" His deep voice managed to pull me all the rest of the way out of my daydream and back into reality.

I blushed. "Sorry, it got too quiet, and I didn't think you'd mind."

I felt frozen as his eyes caught mine, and he moved further into the kitchen. He stopped a couple of inches away, and my breath hitched. "You do that a lot, you know."

I tilted my head. "What?"

"Apologize." He reached out and curled the strand of hair that had fallen loose around my ear.

I shivered.

"Cold?"

I shook my head, still lost in the green depths of his eyes. I chanced a quick glance at his lips and wondered what it would feel like to kiss him. Would it be like the ones I'd experienced in the past? Aggressive? Claiming? Sloppy? Somehow, I didn't think so. Although, I wouldn't be against the first two if it were coming from this man.

"How are you doing?"

The question took me by surprise, and I looked up at him again. What I saw staring back at me might as well have been a bucket of cold water. While I had been imagining what it would be like to have his lips on me, he had been watching me with careful neutrality. There was nothing in those seafoam-green eyes to indicate he was feeling the same way I was.

I cleared my throat and shrugged. "Better. I'm, um, sorry for being such a hassle the last several days."

"You weren't a hassle, Leah."

I blinked. That couldn't have been anger lacing his words, could it?

Deacon yanked open the fridge and pulled out the water jug and a couple of cans of pop. My mind spun as I watched him move around the kitchen, gathering the placemats and cutlery I had set out earlier and then setting the table in the makeshift dining room between the kitchen and living room.

What the hell had I said now?

The oven timer beeped, and I went about removing the chicken and plating it on top of the rice on each plate. Deacon refused to meet my eyes while we ate, and each time I tried to start a conversation, he would reply with one- or two-word answers, never giving me anything to work with.

I exhaled hard and slumped back against the chair, twirling the can on the table between my fingers.

"I'm sorry," I said when the silence became like a thick layer of smoke between us. It was too hard to breathe. "I'm not sure what I did, but I'm —"

"Don't you dare apologize again," Deacon said, interrupting me. He pushed his chair away from the table and turned to face me, resting his elbows on his knees as he sat forward. "I should be the one to apologize. I didn't mean to act like a jerk back there. I have a hard time hearing people I care for talking down about themselves. That's not an excuse, though."

My brain stuttered to a stop. He cared about me. How? Why?

"Why don't I clean up here, and you go get into something warm. I set up the fire pit earlier, and I think I saw all the things for s'mores in the pantry," he suggested with a small smile.

I groaned. "I haven't had s'mores in so long. You have yourself a deal."

I left Deacon to clean up the kitchen from dinner as I went back to the bedroom. His sister had packed a pullover hoodie in the bag she sent for me, but it was too fitted. I wanted something comfortable. Something oversized. Something of Deacon's.

I told myself that wasn't the reason I was going through the sweaters in his closet, but it totally was. I moved clothes aside until I found a worn sweater that still smelled faintly of him. I took it off the hanger and held it briefly under my nose, committing that scent to memory before I pulled it over my head and shoved my arms through. The hem hit just below my knees. Perfect.

Deacon wasn't in the cabin when I emerged from the room. I could see an orange glow from the back window, so I made my way out the back door in the kitchen. Tonight was a particularly chilly one. I cupped my hands over my mouth and blew into them and wondered if the sweater I had chosen would be enough to keep me warm enough.

I'd just have to sit a little closer to the fire if I got too cold. Or maybe Deacon would… No, I couldn't think like that. There was nothing between us. Would never be nothing between us. As far as he was concerned, he was just doing me a favour. Man, that thought stung, but what did I honestly expect? He'd practically found me on the streets and offered to help me. That was not how a romance started. I didn't care what the books and movies said; it didn't work that way. I was kidding myself if I thought I'd ever have a chance with him.

"Hey, I saved you a spot," he said cheekily when he spotted me on the porch.

I laughed and descended the stairs. "How thoughtful of you. Thank you."

"You are welcome."

As soon as I sat in the camping chair to his left, he handed me a stick with a preloaded marshmallow. I accepted gratefully and stuck the bundle of sugar in the flames.

"What are you doing?" Deacon practically shrieked in horror.

I glanced over my shoulder at him, confused. "Roasting my marshmallow. What does it look like?"

He sputtered and pointed at the now on-fire candy. "That is not roasting. That is blasphemy."

I chuckled and blew out the flames. The once snow-white surface was now a charred black. Perfect. "I like it crispy. It adds flavour," I teased as I reached between us to grab a piece of chocolate and graham crackers.

"It's sacrilege is what it is," he muttered, rotating his own stick above the fire so that it was an even brown on all sides.

I rolled my eyes at the precision with which he roasted his marshmallow. I wondered if that was the same precision he took with everything. Would it be the same way he explored the body of the person in his bed? Would his calloused fingers take their time exploring every dip and curve? Would they explore every line? I crossed my legs and clenched my thighs at the phantom feeling of Deacon's fingers ghosting over my body. God, I wanted that. Not even twenty-four hours past detoxing and I was already imagining what it would be like to be under the man. I was going to hell if I hadn't been on my way there already.

He handed me another marshmallow with a skeptical look. I wanted to laugh at the debate that was clearly taking place in his head.

"Deacon, hand me the marshmallow."

I could see the flicker of the flame reflected in his eyes as he lifted a brow. I bit my lip.

"If I give you this sugary goodness, are you going to desecrate it too?"

"Desecrate? Really?"

He watched me silently. It was a little unnerving having the full weight of his attention. I squirmed and uncrossed and crossed my legs again, holding out a hand. "Give it to me."

I didn't know if it was the light of the fire playing tricks on my vision or if it was a blush staining his cheeks when he reluctantly placed the object in question in my palm.

"It's not right," he murmured when I proceeded to set the new marshmallow on fire just like that first one.

When he offered me a third, I shook my head but popped a piece of chocolate in my mouth all the same. I was sugared out. If I ate any more, I wasn't sure I would sleep tonight, and after the last few days, sleep was a special commodity.

I relaxed back in the chair and tipped my head back. The stars were out in full force today, and without all the light pollution of the city, we could actually see them. They were beautiful. I allowed the sounds of the night around us to seep into my bones and settle my racing mind. The stress I had been carrying around the last several years eased too as I listened to the symphony of the crackling fire.

"I never knew my mom."

I had no idea why I blurted that out, but it felt right. I was grateful when Deacon didn't say anything and let me continue sorting through my thoughts as I tried to figure out what I wanted to share with him.

"She fled the hospital hours after giving birth to me. They didn't even know her name. She came into the emergency department in active labour. They barely had time to get her onto a bed before I made my way into the world." I stared into the fire so hard I thought I could almost see the event play out in the yellow-orange flames. "She never wanted me."

"What happened next?" Deacon asked after a moment or two of silence.

"I don't know. I guess they eventually found out who she was and put out a missing person's. A friend of my dad saw it and told him about it." I shrugged and burrowed into the sweater. "He didn't like talking about that part much, but he loved to tell me how my mother didn't want me."

Even though I was on the verge of turning four when he died, I still had very vivid dreams of my dad telling me how my mother abandoned me. I didn't even know if it were possible to remember things from that early on, but the dreams sure felt real.

I yawned and with the warmth of the fire and the ease of Deacon's company I figured I'd close my eyes as I continued telling him about my parents.

Chapter Eleven

Deacon

It felt like I stopped breathing when she began talking about her parents. I didn't want to move or breathe too loud in fear that she may not have continued talking. She needed this. From that very first day in my apartment, I could tell that there was so much she was holding on to.

I was not prepared for what she had said, though. I was angry on her behalf. How dare her father tell her something like that, no matter how true it may have been. Nobody should tell a child that their mother never wanted them.

I wanted to say that maybe she had been better off without them, but I bit my tongue. I had a feeling that wouldn't have gone over well, and when she continued talking, I was glad I hadn't said anything.

"My dad and I lived an okay life. I mean, I think so anyway. He died when I was three…almost four, so maybe we didn't."

"I'm sorry," I said in a low voice.

"Don't be. I was the one who found him, except I didn't know he had died. I just thought he was sleeping on the carpet. Sometimes he fell asleep on the floor in front of the TV when we were playing. I thought…"

A sob escaped her. I reached over and took her hand, giving it a quick squeeze to let her know that she didn't have to go on if it was too painful.

"It was a day or two before anyone found us."

"Fuck. Leah, I —"

The quick shake of her head shut me up. "It's not your fault. You didn't do anything. I hate when people say they're sorry when someone dies. Why? Did they kill them? Are they responsible for the death? If not, then what's the point? It doesn't accomplish anything. It doesn't bring them back or make it easier."

I had a couple of thoughts on the subject, but I didn't voice them. It was obvious that she was still in pain from her dad's passing, and I didn't want to belittle that by starting an argument on the matter. Instead, I let go of her hand momentarily and yanked her chair closer before I wrapped my arm around her shoulders.

"You're right. It doesn't," I murmured into her hair. She smelled like the shampoo I kept in the shower, and a need I never knew I had started to take root in me. I wanted to possess her. To claim her as mine. If she were mine, I would make sure she never experienced the same amount of hurt again. I would spend the rest of my days protecting her.

"Did you ever find your mom?" I closed my eyes and tried to prepare myself for the answer.

"No. I never had the desire to. Still don't. She abandoned me, so why would I want to waste my energy?"

We were both quiet as we contemplated her words. Then she spoke again. "My foster mom was all the mom I needed. She was great. Always singing when she brushed my hair. She would read to me every night too until I fell asleep, and every Saturday morning, she would make pancakes in the shape of my favourite cartoon characters."

I could hear the smile in her voice, even though I couldn't see it.

"What happened to her?"

She swallowed, the sound seeming so loud in the otherwise quiet night. "Cancer. They found it too late. By the time she was diagnosed, she only had a month or two left. After she died, I went back into the system, but you know how it is. Nobody wants a six-year-old with attachment issues."

I had no idea what to say to her after that. So, I didn't say anything. I pulled her closer — or as close as I could with the armrests of each chair in the way — and laid my cheek on the top of her head. I felt her shudder and knew she was crying. We sat in more silence as I held her while she cried it out.

After several minutes, it felt like her breathing had evened out, and when I glanced down, her eyes were closed. I eased her back in her chair and went about putting out the fire. I gathered up the sticks we used for roasting and the extra marshmallows, chocolate, and graham crackers and ran them into the cabin before going back. She stirred only long enough to wrap her arms around my neck when I lifted her up to carry her inside.

I brought her into the bedroom and laid her down

on the side of the bed closest to the door. She looked more peaceful in sleep now than I had seen her the last couple of days.

Good. I hoped it would be a peaceful rest. She needed it.

When I started to step away from the bed, her hand shot out and grabbed my wrist.

Without opening her eyes, she asked, "Stay?"

I warred with myself. I didn't want to take advantage of her. Especially not when she was in this state. But could I just walk away from a request like that?

The answer was no. I couldn't.

I unzipped my hoodie and reached behind my neck to pull off my shirt but kept my sweatpants on. Then I went around the other side of the bed and slipped under the covers. I had resolved myself to sleeping stiffly on my back so that I didn't accidentally reach for her in my sleep.

That went out the window when Leah reached behind her and patted the bed until she found my arm. She tried to lift it and pull me closer to her, but I didn't budge.

"Come on."

Her voice was like a siren in the night, and my body moved without my permission as I curled around her, one arm slung over her waist. As she drifted back off to sleep, I tried not to think about how perfectly we fit together.

THE NEXT MORNING AS WE SAT AROUND THE TABLE eating breakfast while Leah talked about wanting to explore a few of the trails around here before we headed back to the city, I made a promise to myself that I would bring up the possibility of therapy to her. The story she had told me last night had stuck with me, even following me into my dreams, and it was all I could think about in the light of day.

I wanted to call and ask my mom what she thought I should do, but I didn't want to betray Leah's trust, though I trusted my mom unquestionably and knew she wouldn't tell the rest of the family if I asked her not to. I still couldn't risk the little thread of trust Leah had in me to help her through this.

She seemed like she was doing better today. Her eyes were a little brighter; the gold in them had a bit more sparkle than they held when I had first met her. But the pinched lines around her mouth spoke to how much weight from her past she was still carrying around. I was worried that if she didn't address some of those demons and soon, what we accomplished up here would be for nothing.

"Don't get your hopes up, though, D. Forty to sixty percent of all drug addicts will relapse at least once."

My brother's voice echoed in my head as I stared at the cooling eggs on my plate. I hated that he had put that thought in my head, but I also knew that he was probably right. That was why I had hoped that I could convince her to go see someone.

"Are you okay?"

I glanced up from pushing the eggs around my plate and found Leah staring intently at me, her brows furrowed slightly down.

"Have you considered seeing someone?" I blurted and instantly regretted it when a look of hurt crossed her features and she visibly shut down right in front of me. "That didn't come out right."

"No, it's fine. I know what you meant," she said, but the way she jerkily collected her plate and took it to the kitchen belied her words.

I got up and followed her, needing to fix it.

"I just meant that it might help if you found someone to talk to. It's not going get any easier once we leave here and go back to the city."

She slammed her palms down on the counter beside the sink and turned to face me. Fury burned behind her eyes.

"Do you think I don't know that?" She laughed, but it wasn't out of humour. "I've been clean for less than a week, and the thought of using is still there. For every memory that assaults me, the urge to use to make it go away grows tenfold. So, believe me, I know it's only going to get worse. I don't need you to remind me of that."

She was shaking by the time she was done talking, and I didn't think twice about reaching for her and pulling her into my arms, cradling her head into my chest.

"Detoxing isn't the hardest part, Deacon. It's what comes after."

She sniffed, then pulled back only enough so she could look up at my face and kept her arms wrapped around my waist, her hands clutching the material of my T-shirt.

"I don't know if I'm ready to talk to some stranger, though. Especially someone who has no idea what it's like and not when I know they're going to judge me for the choices I made."

I thumbed away the tears that had fallen down her cheeks and cupped her face in my palms. "I promise you nobody's going to judge you, and if they do, they'll have to answer to me."

Logically, I knew I shouldn't have made her that promise, but I'd be damned if I didn't try my hardest to make it true.

She smiled, sad and small, and called me out on my bullshit. "That's sweet of you but not necessary. It's part of the life I led. I'm used to it."

"You shouldn't have to be used to it."

Her eyes dropped to my lips, and her tongue peeked out to lick along her bottom lip. I let out an involuntary groan and tried to step back, but she increased the pressure of her hands at my back. I could've broken away if I really tried. I was stronger than her, and part of me wanted to, but there was another bigger part that wanted to see what she'd do next.

I told myself I wasn't going to pursue her, that I'd keep my growing attraction to her on lockdown until she was ready. But if she made the first move, I wasn't going to stop her.

I saw it happen, was expecting it even, but the warm press of her lips against mine still took me by surprise. I sucked in a breath and pulled her tighter against me, kissing her back. She tasted like eggs and coffee, but I didn't care. She felt good pressed against my body. I wanted to devour her. To make her feel good and wanted and seen.

I picked her up and sat her on the edge of the counter. Her legs fell open to make room for me, and her hands roamed over my back before finding their way down and cupping my ass, pushing me closer.

"Leah," I moaned, trying to catch my breath.

"I want this, Deacon," she said, ghosting her full lips along my jaw to my ear. "Please."

God, that word spilling from her lips undid me, and I couldn't hold back any longer.

"Lean back on your elbows," I said, then hooked my fingers in the waistband of the sweatpants she was wearing and tugged them down. Leah lifted her hips to help me pull the material down. I let the pants fall to the tile at my feet and took a minute to drink her in. I wasn't sure when she'd taken off the shirt she had been wearing, but I didn't give a shit. She was perfection. All naturally tanned skin and curves for days despite her thinner frame from years spent on the streets. I leaned over her, curled a hand around her neck, and pulled her to me for another kiss. It was only our second kiss, but I already couldn't get enough.

I trailed open-mouthed kisses and nips down her throat and along her collarbone. Her head fell back on a moan when I sucked a nipple and flicked my tongue across the hardening bud. I switched and did the same to the other as her hand slid through my hair. She grunted when I took the bud between my teeth and gave it a slight tug. That sound made my quickly hardening dick twitch.

"Feet up on the counter," I instructed and continued my exploration down, dropping to my knees when she complied.

"Oh," she mewled when I pressed kisses to her inside thighs. Her back arched, and she wiggled a little closer to the edge in an attempt to get my mouth closer to where she really wanted it. "Dammit, Dea… ugh, yes!" she exclaimed when my tongue licked up her slit to her clit.

I moaned as her taste hit my tongue. I dove in for more like I had been starving and she was my first meal. I didn't stop until she bucked her hips wildly, pulling at my hair, and whined about being too sensitive.

I got to my feet, grinning at her spread apart on my kitchen counter. I palmed my cock and gave the base a tight squeeze. The sight of her like that was enough to make me come, but I didn't want to just yet. I had to make sure that she was taken care of. I could finish in the shower later.

"C'mere," I said, taking her hands and helping her sit up.

Her eyes were glazed, and a sleepy smile graced her lips. When her hands pushed up my shirt and began exploring my torso, I took her wrists in mine and halted their journey to my waistband.

"You don't want me to return the favour?"

The hurt was back in her eyes, and I had half a mind to let her wrists go so that she could finish me off, but this was for her.

I framed her face again and kissed her deep, savouring the moan that escaped her as she tasted herself on my tongue.

"Believe me, I do," I said when the kiss ended. "But this was for you. You've had a taxing few days, and I want to make you feel good."

"But I want —"

I cut her off with a peck to her lips. "Later," I said. "Go take a bath. I'll clean up here and then join you. If you want."

"I want," she replied, then kissed me before hopping off the counter and heading for the bathroom.

I watched her walk away until the door closed behind her. I tried to feel guilty about what just happened, but I couldn't. Hell, I wanted more of what happened. Next time, I wanted her writhing beneath me, my name spilling from her lips as she came around my cock.

Chapter Twelve

L eah

THE SHOWER CURTAIN WAS PULLED OPEN, INVITING A cool breeze with it. I shivered as a warm body pressed against my back. Deacon reached for the bottle of body wash I'd just taken from the ledge. I had already washed my hair while he was busy cleaning the kitchen. He poured the soap out into his palm and replaced the bottle.

I turned in his arms, my eyes automatically seeking out his. Neither of us looked away as he rubbed his palms together to get a good lather and then proceeded to wash my body with excruciating gentleness. Nobody had ever touched me with such care. Just like in the kitchen, I had no idea what to do with this.

Pain I could handle. Humiliation was nothing new.

But this? I shook with the weight of the unknown and the newness of it all.

"You're so beautiful, Leah," Deacon murmured by my ear as his hands roamed down my waist to my hips and then around to my back.

The dam I had been trying to hold back broke, and I sobbed. Deacon continued washing my body as I cried. He didn't stop to tell me everything was going to be okay. He didn't make me any promises like he had in the kitchen. It was like he somehow knew I didn't need any of that in that moment. Sometimes a girl's just got to cry it out. He gave me the space to do exactly that while still taking care of me.

The more time I spent with this man, the more I wondered how he was still single. Why hadn't someone snagged him up already?

When he reached out to grab the body wash again, I laid a hand on his arm to stop him and then slipped the bottle from his hands. Tears still streamed down my cheeks, mixed with the water from the shower. Neither of us spoke as I copied his movements and squirted the soap in my palms. I rubbed them into a lather and then touched his chest.

He hissed and shivered under my cold hands despite the warm water beating down on us.

"Sorry," I said and started washing him.

"No need to apologize." His voice sounded like gravel in the small room.

I washed his torso and thighs before going to my knees and washing his legs too. When I stood up again, I took him in hand and washed his cock and balls. There was nothing sexual about it. I wanted to take care of him just like he had me. When his front was done, I switched places with him and soaped up his back while he rinsed his front under the steady stream.

When we were both done, he turned the water off and pushed open the curtain. Deacon got out first and held out a towel for me. He wrapped me in the soft, fluffy material when I stepped out, then proceeded to dry me off before roughly drying himself.

Deacon wrapped me back in the towel, then picked me up and carried me bridal-style back to his room.

"I can walk," I protested, even as my arms curled around his neck, and I buried my nose in his throat. He smelled like a dark storm brewing, and I loved it.

"I know," he replied with no further explanation.

When we entered the bedroom, he stood me up, then went over to the dresser and pulled open the top drawer, rummaging through it until he pulled out a pair of boxers and a T-shirt. I raised a questioning brow but didn't give voice to the question as he continued to dress me in his clothes.

"We just woke up not too long ago," I argued when he moved to draw back the covers.

"I'm aware. I thought we could spend the day under the covers watching movies." He blushed, and I wondered not for the first time what this man was doing here with me. He could be spending his time with anyone else.

I crawled onto the bed and shifted until I sat with my back against the headboard and pillows and pulled the duvet over my lap. When I was settled in the big bed, Deacon donned a clean pair of sweats and then disappeared out the door. I heard cupboards opening and closing from the crack in the door. Packets crinkled as they were opened, and the fridge opened and closed before everything fell silent.

He reappeared a couple of minutes later with a tray in his hands. Chocolate, fruit, cheese, meats, and crackers decorated it in a makeshift charcuterie board. Out of his pockets, he pulled a couple of bottles of black cherry sparkling water and sat them in the middle of the bed with the tray before joining me on his side of the bed.

I popped a milk chocolate in my mouth and grinned. This felt good. Too good.

"Alright," he said, rearranging the duvet across his lap and moving the tray closer so that we didn't have to reach far for the food. "I showed you my favourite movie. It's only fair you tell me yours."

I beamed. It wasn't every day you found out that a grown man's favourite movie was *Brave*.

I gave him a sheepish look as I fiddled with the edge of the covers. I hoped he wouldn't judge me for my taste in movies. I wasn't like other women. I didn't love cheesy rom-coms or animated movies. I mean, don't get me wrong, I liked them, but I wouldn't consider them a favourite. Blow shit up movies were where it was at for me.

"*The Expendables*," I said in a low voice.

Deacon paused with a cube of marble cheese halfway to his mouth. He turned his head to me, his eyes ping-ponging between mine, and then he just nodded, popped the cube between his lips and pulled up his Netflix account. That was it. No shock at the reveal of my favourite movie of all time. No teasing that I was a woman, therefore my choice should've been something romantic. No judgement.

I sat back with a smile on my face and pulled my legs up so my feet were planted on the mattress. As the opening scene played out and Barney and Christmas appeared on screen, I breathed out a sigh. It had been a long time since I had seen this movie. Too long.

Deacon and I continued to pick away at the food for the first bit of the movie, but eventually, even he had gotten too into it to pay attention to the food. So, he moved it to the floor beside the bed and lifted his arm in a silent invitation for me to snuggle closer.

"Why *The Expendables*?" he asked after a while.

"Why *Brave*?" I countered, keeping my eyes on the movie.

His fingers traced lazy patterns on my arm as he answered. "She reminds me of my sister. She doesn't need a knight in shining armour or a prince to save her. Lilah was... is the same way. Even though she had four brothers who had her back, she didn't need us to fight her battles or make everything better."

"She's strong."

He grunted. "Maybe too strong. She doesn't lean on anyone. We used to think that was a good thing — she'd never be reliant on anyone. But as time went on, the four of us realized that Lilah never talked to anyone. Not even our parents. She's gotten so good at putting on a smile when she's around us, I don't think any of us would know if it were fake."

"You're worried about her. That she might explode when it gets to be too much," I observed, my fingers twirling in the little bit of hair on his chest. I resisted the urge to tug on the bars in his nipples, but only just.

"Well, it hasn't happened so far. Though, there's nothing wrong with admitting to needing help every now and then. I just hope that she knows she can come to us."

We watched the rest of the movie in silence, and I

was embarrassed to find that I almost drifted off multiple times throughout it. The comforting sounds of the movie combined with the warmth of Deacon's body was perfectly conducive to early afternoon naps.

"So," he started, reaching for the remote, "your turn."

I looked up at him, confused, until I realized he had been referring to me having avoided the question of why this was my favourite movie. I laughed.

"It's not as deep as you may think," I said.

"Doesn't matter."

"I liked the plot," I answered and raised a brow, hoping he'd get my meaning.

He did.

Deacon threw his head back and laughed. God, that sound. If comfort had a feeling, it would be Deacon's arms. If it had a sound, it would be his laugh. It reminded me of long-ago family dinners when my foster mom was still alive. One year, her brother had come over, and we were all gathered in the living room. He told the funniest stories that would have us laughing all night. That was one of the last good memories I had before she died, and everything changed.

"Another one?" Deacon asked, pulling me from my memories. He already had the second movie pulled up and was waiting for my answer.

I rolled my eyes. "Like I'd ever say no to more Statham."

WE SPENT THE NEXT COUPLE OF DAYS COOKING breakfast together and then exploring the various hiking trails in the area before coming back to the cabin and watching movies in bed for the rest of the day.

Deacon hadn't touched me again since that day, and I had no idea what to think about it. Was he ashamed about what we did? I tried not to let it get to me, but I would be lying if I said it didn't.

I hummed to myself in the kitchen while I gathered all the fixings for sandwiches. We had decided that today would be our last day in solitude before we headed back to the city. A part of me was excited to go back, to be part of society again, but the other part was terrified. I had come up with multiple excuses as to why we should stay here, away from all the temptation. I had an answer for every possible thing Deacon could throw at me as to why we couldn't hide away for a bit longer. I never voiced any of them. I knew it wouldn't be healthy to avoid real life for much longer.

The song on the radio switched over to Lee Brice, and I swayed my hips to the beat as I sang along to the words and spread mayo on the four slices of bread. Deacon's large body pressed against my back, and his long arm wrapped around my waist as he reached out to slip the knife from mine and placed it down on the counter, then snagged my wrist and spun me around.

Deacon's hair was still wet from his shower. I followed a bead of water down the side of his throat until it disappeared under the collar of his black T-shirt.

"Wh-what are you doing?" I asked breathlessly.

"What kind of gentleman would I be if I let a beautiful woman dance by herself," he said and pulled me into his body.

"Where'd you learn to dance?" I asked as he moved us around the kitchen, spinning me out and pulling me back a couple of times.

"My parents were big ballroom dancers. My dad would take my mom out every weekend to a club. He hated dancing, but it made her happy, so he did it. When us boys were old enough, we all took lessons. To practise, we'd find random moments to pull our mom or Lilah into a dance. It kinda became our thing."

That was probably the sweetest thing I'd ever heard.

He sounded embarrassed by having admitted that, though, but I told him how sweet I thought it was. The song drew to an end, and Deacon spun me once more, then dipped me after spinning me back. I couldn't stop the laugh that bubbled out. I threw my arms around his neck as he righted me and hugged him, thankful to him for taking my mind off having to go back to real life tomorrow, but also for everything he'd done for me.

"Thank you," I said into his neck.

His arms tightened around me for a moment, and then he let me go. "You're welcome."

He framed my face in his palms, and I thought he was going to kiss me for the first time since the other day, but he didn't. His thumbs traced the apples of my cheeks, and he stared intently into my eyes. He looked like he wanted to say something but then thought better of it.

"Deacon, I —" I started to call out when he turned.

He paused on his way back out to the living room.

Deacon, I, what? I want a repeat of what happened in here a couple days ago, and I'm hoping you do too? I want to stay here because yes, I'm terrified of relapsing, but I'm more terrified that you're going to walk away and pretend like this week never happened. I swallowed hard and shook my head.

"Never mind."

He went back to the living room and turned on the TV while I finished making our lunches. After we ate, we lounged on the couch. The early spring sunlight provided a false sense of warmth as it streamed through the open curtains. Even though I had hoped we could explore more of the attraction that simmered between us, this would still go down as one of the best years of my life.

Chapter Thirteen

Leah

Deacon's apartment was the exact same as I remembered it. It was light and airy; the walls painted an off-white with green plants in different corners that lent pops of colour. It looked like something from a social media ad and not all like a bachelor suite.

As if already anticipating my question, Deacon huffed, hiking the strap of his duffle bag higher on his shoulder. He brought all his clothes home this time so that he could wash them since the cabin didn't have a washing machine or dryer.

"My sister," he said by way of explanation.

"I like it." I stood awkwardly in the entryway, not sure whether I should be following him or what he expected me to do now that we were back.

Truthfully, if he kicked me out, I had nowhere to go. I was afraid that I would have to return to tent city. Even as I thought it, I knew it wasn't an option. I didn't care what I had to do; I wouldn't be returning there. I'd find a good shelter and try to get work so I could get my own place. I would not waste the opportunity Deacon afforded me.

Something soft pressed itself against my leg and wound itself between my feet. I glanced down to the cat I'd only gotten a glimpse of before. It was tiny. It's orange fur was interspersed with white. Blue eyes looked up at me, pleading for me to cuddle it. How could I possibly say no to that face? I bent to pick up the cat and it immediately snuggled into my chest with a loud purr.

"Hey," Deacon called, coming back down the hallway. "I thought you were right behind me."

"I, um, wasn't sure if you wanted me to follow you or if I should just go," I answered, scratching behind Lumière's ear.

He smiled when he saw his cat in my arms then cocked his head, brows furrowed. "Do you have anywhere to go?"

There wasn't any malicious intent in the question, but it stung all the same. I shook my head.

"Then you can stay in the guest bedroom until you get your feet under you. C'mon."

Disappointment blazed a fire through my veins when he suggested the guest bedroom, although it shouldn't have surprised me. We weren't anything, and that day at the cabin could be chalked up to relieving stress. Nothing else. Even though I wanted more.

Deacon took the bag from my shoulder and headed down the hall. This time, I followed him. We stopped at the door before where I knew the master bedroom was from my previous visit. The room was a good size. A queen bed sat in one corner across from the door. A La-Z-Boy chair took up the corner beside the door, and on the far wall was a tallboy dresser. The room was decorated much like the rest of the apartment but in cool blue tones instead of the pops of green created by the plants.

"I had my brothers clean this out and move my office stuff to a storage unit for now. I hope the bed is comfortable. If not, we can look for another one."

"I'm not just going to live here for free," I blurted when Deacon stopped talking and dropped the bag on the bed.

He turned. "Leah, you know I don't expect any payment."

"I know you don't, but I don't want to be a freeloader. Not anymore," I added, then looked away for a moment, thinking about what I could offer him in return for letting me stay here. "Let me at least help out around here. I can cook and clean around the apartment." I'd do anything, I was that desperate not to go back.

"Leah," he breathed, exasperated.

"Please," I begged.

Deacon sighed, pinching the bridge of his nose between thumb and forefinger. "Okay, fine. But I don't expect you to pick up after me when I'm home."

I struck out my hand. "Deal."

Deacon grinned, amused, but took my offered hand in his. "Deal."

He left me to unpack my bag and get settled in what was now my room. It still felt surreal to think that I had a room to myself. One whose four walls weren't made of nylon.

As I put the little bit of clothes in the dresser and

small closet, I made a mental note to ask Deacon where the local Salvation Army was so that I could get a few more articles of clothes, especially if I wanted to find a job. Which I did. Once everything was put away and the bag stowed on the top shelf in the closet, I grabbed some clean clothes and headed for the bathroom across the hall.

I groaned internally at the sight of the sunken bathtub. I was definitely going to take advantage of that one day. Maybe when Deacon was at work so that I didn't have to worry about taking too long. I turned on the water to the shower, making sure it was the right temperature, then stripped and stepped inside, pulling the door closed behind me.

A sigh escaped me as the hot water loosened muscles I had no idea had been tense till now. I turned my back to the stream and tipped my head forward, my long hair falling in a curtain around my face, allowing the water to hit my neck and shoulders. I'd never take showers for granted again.

Not wanting to waste the hot water, I quickly shampooed and conditioned my hair, then washed my body and rinsed. The towel was warm when I grabbed it from the bar, and I realized it must be heated. I wanted to burrow into the fluffy material but settled for wrapping it around my body.

I swiped a hand across the mirror to wipe away the fog and startled at my reflection. I hardly recognized the woman who stared back at me. Over the last week, I had put on some weight. My cheeks weren't as gaunt, and my collarbone not as pronounced. I still had a long way to go before it didn't look like a gust of wind could blow me away, but it was a definite improvement.

My brown eyes didn't look as dull as they had a week

ago either. There was a spark in them again that I looked forward to flaming into something brighter. Deacon had been a huge help in getting me here, but it was up to me to keep going. I couldn't rely on him for the rest of my life. I wouldn't want to either. If I had any hope of convincing him to give whatever this was a chance, then I had to prove to not just him but myself that I could stand confidently on my own two feet.

That means taking his advice and going to therapy, the little voice at the back of my head said.

I couldn't ignore it this time. It was right. Detox was only a small piece of my recovery journey. If I wanted to stay clean, get my shit together, and not allow the ghosts of my past to control my actions, then I needed to exorcise them once and for all.

I quickly toweled off and dragged a comb through my hair. I reached for the clothes I'd brought with me and cursed when I realized I had forgotten a shirt. Wrapping the towel around my body again, I picked up the bundle of clothes and poked my head out the door. I could hear the TV going in the living room down the hall. Confident that Deacon wouldn't randomly walk by, I dashed out of the bathroom with my head down and bumped into something just outside my door.

I bounced back with an oomph, but before I could go down, strong hands gripped my arms and held me up.

"I'm so sorry. I should've been looking where I was going." I bit my lip and looked up at Deacon's face.

His jaw was clenched, and if I hadn't spent the last week with him, I would've thought he looked almost annoyed, but something blazed to life behind his eyes. Something very similar to that day. My belly clenched, and I had to take a small step back, or chances were good I would've thrown myself at him.

I curled my hair behind my ear and asked him if he needed anything. His answer was a grunted no, and then he stepped around me and closed the bathroom door behind him.

Well, that wasn't awkward at all.

Chapter Fourteen

Deacon

If I hadn't known better, I would be sure that Leah was trying to kill me. I could still feel her in my arms hours later as I lay in bed on my back and stared up at the ceiling.

Fuck, she had smelled so good.

While we were away at the cabin, my sister had dropped off a bunch of stuff for Leah, including shampoo, conditioner, and body wash, all of which smelled incredible. I made a mental note to send a thank-you basket to Lilah that included all of her favourite things. I was going to go all out and didn't care about the cost. She deserved it.

I groaned at the image of Leah wrapped in a towel, her hair still wet and dripping over her shoulder.

The last couple of days at the cabin had been a test in self-control. Every time I got near to her, I wanted to spread her out on the nearest surface and have my way with her again. Only the reminder of why we were up there in the first place had stopped me. I hated feeling like I had somehow taken advantage of her when she was vulnerable.

The look she gave me in the hallway, though, said different. I knew that if I were to have kissed her right then, she would've been okay with it. But consent wasn't something I was willing to guess at. So, until I had her explicit go-ahead, I wouldn't be touching her again, no matter how painful it was going to be.

My phone rang from its spot on the bedside table, and the sigh that escaped me was a mix of relief and annoyance.

"What do you want?" I asked, already knowing who was on the other end.

"Is that any way to speak to your favourite sister?" Lilah's voice came through the line.

"You're my only sister," I volleyed back.

Lilah scoffed. I grinned. My sister may have been closer to Dash in age, but she and I were closer relationship-wise. She'd always be my Pinkie, a nickname I'd given her because she carried a tiny pink blanket everywhere she went from the time she learned how to crawl until she started first grade — the same pink blanket I gave her the day she was born.

"So, how's it going?"

I blew out a fast breath and curled an arm under my head. "It's going," I replied.

"Uh-oh. What'd you do?"

"What makes you think I did anything?" I asked, mock offended.

"D…" she said in her mom voice.

She was twelve years younger than me. How the fuck did she always get me to talk so easily? I relented and told her everything — from what happened at the cabin right down to bumping into a nearly naked Leah in the hallway not fifteen minutes ago. My sister was silent for a few beats before her laughter floated through the phone.

"Why are you laughing?"

"You like her," she managed to say between bouts of laughter. "I'm sorry. I just never thought I'd see the day after —" She stopped talking abruptly, and I was glad. I never wanted to hear that name again.

"Not helping."

"Tell me one thing, D. Why are you avoiding things with her? If you want her, then pursue her."

"She's not ready for anything, Lilah."

"Bullshit," my sister said. "She's a grown-ass woman, Deacon Rutherford. If she wasn't ready, she'd let you know. Leah has lived through experiences we can only imagine. She's had to be strong for a very long time. I'm positive that if you did something she didn't like, she'd have no issues telling you or popping you one. Don't be that asshole and assume you know what she wants. Fucking ask her."

It shouldn't surprise anyone that the minute I could, I spilled my guts to Delilah about Leah. Our brothers didn't even know about Leah. Although, I was sure Lilah was dying to tell them. I was surprised she'd lasted this long without running her mouth.

I lay there, stunned at having been put in my place by my baby sister. But she had a point. I was so worried that I'd do something that could cause Leah to relapse that I didn't stop to think about what she wanted. At no point while we were at the cabin did she indicate that she wasn't happy when we'd cuddle in bed to watch a movie or when my hand lingered a little too long on her arm. Or when I kissed her.

"Did you just last-name me?" I asked in an attempt to stop my mind from wandering back to that day.

She huffed in frustration. "After all of that, that's what you took away?"

I chuckled. "I'm kidding."

"Mhm," she hummed. "So, what are you going to do?"

"I'm going to shoot my shot." I cringed as the words left my lips. I hated that saying.

Lilah whooped, and I had to move the phone away from my ear or risk hearing loss. We talked for a few minutes. She updated me on the adventures my niece and nephew got up to while I was away. When I asked about her husband, she got real quiet, which had my big-bro senses sitting up and taking notice, but I let it go. For now.

"Oh, by the way," she said when we were getting ready to hang up, "Mom expects you two at brunch next weekend!" She sounded so proud of herself as she singsonged that last part.

"Delilah!"

"Sorry, not sorry! She cornered me. What was I supposed to do?"

"Lie," I said. "Stall. Literally anything than what I'm sure you did."

On second thought, maybe she didn't deserve that basket.

"Whatever," she huffed, not sounding the least bit sorry. "It was going to happen sooner or later since you two are living together now. I have to go. I love you."

She was gone before I had a chance to reply. Fucking great. I was going to kill my sister the next time I saw her. Or better yet… I grinned and chuckled evilly. I knew the perfect way to get back at her.

Chapter Fifteen

Leah

Deacon went back to work the next day. He said he would've liked an extra day to make sure I got settled back into the city okay but had to go check on all the sights and see how the progress on the rock walls was coming.

I was fine with it. I didn't want him to feel like he had to babysit me. Plus, I didn't feel much like going out yet anyway. But a few hours after he'd left, I found myself pacing the length of the apartment. I was antsy. I had already cleaned the bathroom and kitchen. Swept and mopped the floors. Dusted the living room and put on a load of laundry.

I tried vegging on the couch with Lumière and pulled up one of his streaming services, but there were too many options, and soon I found myself overwhelmed.

Deacon had given me an old phone last night so that if I needed to get in touch with him during the day for any reason, I could. I downloaded the messenger app I used to use almost immediately, but now as I pulled it out of my pocket, I hesitated.

I knew they would be worried about me, but I wasn't sure if contacting them was the smartest idea either. But not letting them know I was okay was selfish too.

I sat back on the couch and leaned on the arm as I folded my legs up beside me and pulled up the app. Skeet and Mav's contact info had already been saved in the contacts from the last time I had a phone. I opened the group chat we had and sent a quick message letting them know I was alive and okay. Then before either of them could reply, I turned notifications to silent and closed out of the app. The temptation to see if Skeet had met up with his dealer again was too much now that we were back in the city.

Minutes later a phone rang. It took me a bit to realize that it was coming from the landline in the kitchen Deacon used to buzz guests into the building. I bit my lip as I considered whether or not I should pretend that nobody was home. Deacon didn't tell me that he was expecting anyone to come over while he'd be at work so I wasn't sure who would be coming around.

The ringing stopped and I breathed out a relieved breath and relaxed back into the couch. It started up again seconds later. Figuring I should at least see who it was, I got up and went to the kitchen.

"Hello?"

"Leah! Thank God, your home. It's Lilah, Deacon's sister. I brought over some groceries and was worried I'd have to haul them all the way home. Do you mind buzzing me up?"

I frowned but did as she asked. I couldn't very well turn Deacon's sister away from his apartment. I was grateful that I had decided to throw on a pair of leggings and sweater earlier. My hair was still up in the bun I'd thrown it in the night before, but it was too late to change it now. I was pretty sure I could barely pass as presentable. I hoped Lilah didn't mind too much.

She knocked on the door a couple minutes later and I helped her bring in the bags of groceries.

"Ugh, thank you so much. I knew I should've taken the car from Travis this morning, but I hadn't planned on running over here after work," she said, dumping the bags on the kitchen counter. It was only when she put her purse down beside them that she looked at me.

Her dirty-blonde hair hung pin-straight over her shoulders. Her green blouse made the green flecks in her honey eyes pop. She was beautiful.

"Wow," she whispered, her gaze still trained on me.

I squirmed and pulled at the hem of the sweater. "I'm sorry. If I knew you were coming I would've changed."

"No. No, that's not it. Deacon was right. You are gorgeous."

I blushed. *Deacon said I was gorgeous?*

"I'm sorry. I made you embarrassed." She giggled. "Would you mind helping me unpack all these and then we can have some tea? I need to sit down for a few minutes before I head back out. These heels are killing my feet."

"Yeah, sure." I jumped in and helped her put things away, only mildly shocked at how much there actually was. Did Deacon not do his own shopping? Somehow I didn't think that was right seeing as how he seemed to do a pretty good job when we went grocery shopping for the cabin.

"Sorry about all of that. I swear sometime our mom forgets that her boys are grown-ups and can take care of themselves," Lilah explained as we put the last of it away and she moved for the kettle.

"Your mom sent all that?"

Lilah nodded, reaching up to grab a couple mugs in the top cupboard. "Kinda. She knew D was back at work today and that I was getting off early so she called and harassed me until I agreed to pick up a few things for him. Told me she'd send me a list."

I laughed when she turned to me and rolled her eyes dramatically before turning back to drop tea bags in each cup and added water from the kettle.

"Thank you," I said when she handed me one.

I followed her to the couch. Lumière immediately hopped up beside me and kneaded my thigh before curling up beside me and going back to sleep.

"He likes you."

"I like the little guy too. We've gotten plenty of cuddles the last couple days." I reached down to pet him, eliciting a loud purr of approval.

Lilah laughed. "Lumière too, but I meant my brother."

"Oh." I ducked my head to hide another blush and concentrated on smoothing down Lumière fur like it was the most interesting thing on Earth.

"So, um, how are you doing if you don't mind me asking?"

Her question took me by surprise for a second, but it shouldn't have. Of course, Deacon must have told her about me. I wondered if he'd told the rest of his family too.

"I don't mean to pry," Lilah hurriedly added. "D and I are close, so he confided in me. I hope that's okay? He hasn't told anyone else about you." Her eyes grew wide as the realization of what she said dawned. I had to suppress a smile. "I mean, not that he doesn't want to tell people about you. I just meant—"

I cut her off before went into a full panic. "It's fine. I honestly expected him to tell all of you."

She shook her and pulled her legs up under her. "D's loyal like that. He won't say a word until you're ready and comfortable with the family knowing. I mean, they know you exist, but that's about it. I mean, he hasn't even told me everything."

I nodded absently. A little comforted that he hadn't told everyone my sob story. I took a sip of my tea so that I wouldn't be tempted to chew on my lip. I found myself wanting to tell Lilah everything. I'd only just met her, but when I thought about telling her my story, I didn't become a ball of anxiety like I usually did. I felt almost at peace with it.

So I did. Over the next hour, I told Lilah everything. I told her about my parents. About my first foster mom. About her dying and then hopping from one foster home to another until I was sixteen. I told her about the events that led up to me discovering and using heroin for the first time, and then my fall into addiction.

By the time I was done, tears streamed down both our cheeks. Lilah pulled me into her arms and squeezed.

"I'm not going to say I'm sorry for everything you had to go through because I'm sure you've heard it before."

I laughed then sniffed as I wiped away a tear.

"But I am going to tell you how strong I think you are because I'm pretty sure you haven't heard it enough.

What you went through," she paused and shook her head. "I couldn't even imagine."

I swallowed hard and thanked her in a faint voice. She was right. Nobody had told me how strong they thought I was. It'd always been the opposite. It was refreshing and also a little odd to not hear someone tell me I was a failure.

We talked for a bit more. Lilah told me stories about how it was growing up with five older brothers. Soon enough she had to leave so that she could cook dinner for her kids since her husband, Travis, was working the last shift tonight. She promised she would stop by again later this week then she left.

I turned the TV on again and picked a random show on a random channel to watch while I gnawed the shit out of my thumbnail. My brain kept replaying the entire conversation with Lilah, going over every microscopic detail until I was driving myself crazy.

When an hour or so went by and I no longer felt the need to die of embarrassment, I relaxed into the couch and paid more attention to the show that was on TV. They must have had a marathon on because it was the same show I had put on hours ago. I didn't make it halfway through the episode before my eyes started to droop, and I fell asleep curled up on the couch.

THE SUN HAD ALREADY STARTED TO SET WHEN I WOKE UP from my impromptu nap. A quick glance at the clock above the bookcase told me I had maybe less than an hour before Deacon would be home. That should be enough time to throw together some spaghetti.

I wasn't the greatest cook in the world, but I wasn't

bad either. I was decent. Before the cancer took her, my foster mom tried to teach me everything she knew in the kitchen. I was pretty sure it was because that was the only time I wasn't fidgeting or my imagination wasn't running wild. It was the one time everything slowed down and I could focus.

I used to have dreams of being a baker and opening my own bakery or café one day. Those dreams died alongside her. With no one to teach me or encourage me, there was no point in holding on to them, a fact that was cemented in stone when I found myself living on the streets at sixteen. There was no way I could go to culinary school if I'd never finished high school.

I got the meat sauce simmering on the stove and the spaghetti noodles boiling in a pot of water when I decided that I wanted to surprise Deacon with some dessert. The one thing my foster mom could never resist — mostly I think because she taught me how to make them — were my mini banana chocolate chip muffins. What made mine different from hers was that I drizzled caramel sauce over the top of mine after they came out of the oven.

Deacon had everything I needed for the muffins, including ripe bananas in his freezer. I pulled them out and put them in a Ziploc bag, then filled a sink with warm water and submerged the bananas. Hopefully they'd be thawed in time. They should only need five minutes.

I had just put the muffins in the oven when keys jingled in the front door and Deacon entered the apartment. My jaw dropped. The brown Carhartt work pants hugged his ass perfectly, while the white T-shirt stretched across his chest, accentuating his biceps. The light colour didn't hide his belly, and I loved that. Hard bodies held no appeal for me. I liked to cuddle and not feel like I was snuggled up beside a brick wall. Deacon's arms were perfect too. He was covered in dust and grime as he toed off his work boots and hung his keys on the hook.

He stopped when he moved further into the living area and caught sight of me in the kitchen. A slow grin tugged at the corners of his lips, and I think I melted. Just a little.

"Dinner's ready," I squeaked.

"Awesome. I'm starving. Do you mind if I grab a quick shower first?"

"Not at all. I'll get everything ready for when you get out."

His grin turned into a full smile, and he turned for the hallway but stopped and looked back over his shoulder.

"Thank you, Leah."

I wanted to say that he didn't have to thank me, but before I could, he'd already disappeared down the hall and into the bathroom.

I got the spaghetti plated and placed on the dining room table and was just getting ready to pull the muffins out of the oven when the bathroom door opened.

The apartment wasn't very big. Hints of sandalwood and vanilla floated on the cloud of steam that escaped the bathroom when he stepped out. Thank fuck he was fully dressed. I think I would've swallowed my tongue and burnt the muffins if he had been naked. But a girl could dream.

I had to turn away when he flashed me a grin as he walked through the living room, running a towel through his hair. I focused on putting on the oven mitts and removing the mini muffin tray from the oven, then turned it off.

"This all smells so good," Deacon complimented, tossing the towel over the arm of the couch.

"I hope you like it. I didn't have many opportunities to cook, but I make a mean spaghetti." I smiled, placing the muffins on a rack to cool, then tossed the mitts on the counter.

Deacon laughed and pulled out my chair as I approached the dining table. "Well, I'm sure it's better than what I could do."

"You don't cook?" I asked, surprised.

"Not unless it can be thrown on the grill or in the microwave. What you saw at the cabin was the extent of it." He chuckled on his way to the kitchen to grab us some drinks and came back. "My family makes fun of me for it all the time."

"You're close with them?" I accepted the bottle of water with a grateful smile and twisted open the cap.

"Very. Our parents made sure of it. There was nothing more important than family. That's not to say that we didn't fight because we definitely did," he said, twirling his fork in his spaghetti. "With six kids, it was inevitable. But there's no one I trust more."

"I can't even imagine that."

"Were there no other kids at the foster homes?"

I stared down at my plate and shook my head. "The first foster home I was sent to, I was the only kid. It was nice. I didn't have to compete for anything. The others, not so much. You were lucky if you got an actual bed and not just a flimsy mattress on the floor in a shared room with three other kids."

"When did you…"

"Start living on the streets?" I asked when it was obvious he wasn't going to. "Ten days after my sixteenth birthday."

I bit my lip as I decided exactly how much I was willing to tell him. He'd told me about his family, though, so I thought it only fair I share a bit more about myself. Even if I hated thinking about my time in that foster home.

"The last home I was in, I don't think I ever felt safe. When you hear horror stories about foster homes, it's usually because the dad did something horrible."

"But that wasn't the case with them?"

Deacon had stopped eating, and I had given up the facade of being hungry.

"No." My voice sounded small, haunted, in the open space, and I hated it. I sat up straighter and tried to project as much strength in my voice the next time I spoke. "No one ever talks about just how horrible the mom can be. Maybe even more so. The last one was worse than Ms. Hannigan and Cinderella's stepmother combined."

I winced at a particularly dark time. One of the other girls was being attacked by a couple of the boys who also lived in the house. Ms. Tomson didn't bat an eye when she walked past the open door to the room. She'd always hated how much more attention that girl got than her, even if that attention was negative. I spent the rest of the night curled in a ball on my mattress while the girl's cries echoed through the thin wall. The guilt at not stopping it still ate at me.

"Hey," Deacon's voice cut through the memory. "You did nothing wrong," he said like he could see inside my head.

"I should've done something to help her. Instead, I got up the next day and ran."

I knew that if I didn't get out of there, there was a chance I would be next. I often wondered what happened to that girl. If she got out. I considered tracking her down when I had gotten my feet under me, but I didn't know her last name, and living on the street wasn't really conducive to tracking someone down.

"Maybe, but you can't play the what-if game. Nothing good ever comes of it."

"Yeah," I croaked. "Maybe."

"I have an idea. You in?" he asked, a mischievous grin pulling at the corners of his lips.

"That depends. What are we doing?" I raised a brow.

He laughed. "It wouldn't be a surprise if I told you. C'mon. We'll pack some of those mini muffins for the road."

Deacon picked up our plates and took them to the kitchen. He scraped the leftover food in the garbage and then loaded the dishwasher. I couldn't help but watch him as he moved around the space without a care. It was like nothing I told him affected him. I didn't know what to make of that. There wasn't any judgement when I had finished telling him about one of my biggest regrets, just understanding.

It still got a bit chilly outside in the evenings, so I grabbed a leather jacket Deacon's sister must have dropped off when we were at the cabin. He was already waiting for me at the front door in jeans and a long-sleeved button-up when I emerged from the guest room. We took the elevator to the underground parking garage and then climbed into his truck. Literally. I had to use the running board, and even then, I had to pull myself up. The thing was a beast.

I was sure that it had mostly been custom-built for him and his business. The inside was an all-black leather interior that was buttery soft. The display screen in the middle was all digital, as well as the temperature controls for the air and heated seats. The cab was roomy too. Big but not spaceship big.

I turned the heat for my seat on low and then relaxed back while he maneuvered the monster out of the garage and into traffic. As we left downtown and started toward the outskirts, I grew antsy. I wasn't a super fan of surprises. I rested my elbow on the passenger door and bit my thumb.

"Stop it," Deacon said, but there was amusement in his voice.

"Just tell me what we're doing," I whined, then twisted in my seat so I faced him.

He laughed. "You're hating this, aren't you?"

"So much."

His hair looked more salt than pepper in the passing streetlights. It made me wonder about the things he had seen not just while on deployment, but life in general.

His shoulders shook as he tried to rein in his laughter, but he eventually gave in. "Ever been axe throwing?"

I blanched. "Like real axes? Throwing real axes?"

There was no way.

"Real axes," he confirmed.

"Is that safe?"

Deacon turned a blinding grin on me. I was suddenly glad that we were driving and he had to focus back on the road. "Fairly safe. Just don't let go when you rear back."

"Oh my god," I groaned, straightening in the seat. "We're going to die. I'm going to kill us both."

He chuckled and reached out a hand to squeeze my knee. I think I stopped breathing.

"It's going to be fine. You might even have fun."

"Pssh, says you."

Truth be told, I was excited. I'd never done anything like this before and was looking forward to it, even if I was terrified one or both of us would be leaving without a limb.

Deacon pulled up outside a nondescript building. The parking lot was fairly full. I guessed a lot of people considered axe throwing a great way to spend a Monday night. He managed to find a parking spot close to the entrance just as someone else was leaving. Now that we were here, I wondered if I could come up with an excuse for us to leave.

My time was up before I could come with something. Deacon jogged around the front of the truck and pulled open my door.

"Come on," he said, holding out a hand and helping me out of the truck.

"You know it isn't too late to go bowling or indoor minigolf. Or hell, I'd even take paintball. No?" I asked when he just smiled and shook his head. "Fiiine."

"Are you always like this?"

"Only when it comes to throwing dangerous weapons," I conceded and stepped through the glass door as he held it open.

The place was busy. On the far side and running the whole length of the building were about ten cage-like lanes. There were eight or nine feet high chain-link fences around each of them. Eight of the cages were currently occupied. To our immediate right was the front desk, and to our left, the bathrooms. On the other side of the front desk was what looked like a pub-style restaurant.

"They don't serve alcohol here," Deacon said, leaning down to speak close to my ear. His palm pressed into the small of my back. "I called to double-check before we left."

Even if they had served alcohol, it would've been fine. I never had an issue with drinking; it was opioids that were my drug of choice. But it was sweet that he took the time to make sure I'd be comfortable.

"Thank you."

The couple in front of us finished paying and headed off to one of the empty lanes. Deacon and I stepped up then. The guy at the desk looked young. I seriously doubted whether this would work out.

"Hi. We have a booked time at eight. Deacon Rutherford."

The kid clicked some buttons on the computer and then slid two clipboards across the desk. "I need you to fill these out."

I didn't bother reading the liability form before I signed at the bottom and slid it back, knowing that if I had taken the time to read it, I would've for sure backed out. I didn't miss the crooked smile on Deacon's face either. Once both forms were signed and Deacon had paid the fee, the kid let us know which cage we'd be using for the next hour and that our expert would meet us over there to go over the rules.

"I thought we could throw first and then stop for something to eat. Then you can decide if you want to go again or if it's not your thing," Deacon said, guiding me toward the cage that we had booked for the next hour.

As we neared the cage, out of the corner of my eye I saw a man get ready to throw his next axe, but it completely missed the target and bounced off the chain-link fence next to it.

"Or," I said, cataloguing the exits, "we say we did

and don't. If we leave now, we can catch the beginning of *The Big Bang Theory* marathon."

"Just give it a try. Please."

I swore he pouted and even pulled out the puppy eyes.

"For me," he added, and I was done for.

There was no way I could say no to that face.

"Okay, fine. One hour, but only if you promise not to get anywhere near me while I'm holding it."

"Uh, that was kinda the plan," Deacon teased, and I playfully slapped his chest.

"Alright, smartass."

We'd just taken off our coats and hung them on a nearby available hook when someone joined us at the cage. She was older than the kid at the front desk, but it didn't look like she would be able to lift an axe above her head, let alone haul one down the cage. Then again, neither did I, so what did I know.

"Hi, I'm Katie. I'll be your instructor today. I'm assuming this is your first time?" she said in a bubbly voice.

I wanted to roll my eyes but didn't want to appear rude to the person whose responsibility was to show me how to throw a sharp weapon.

"No," I said at the same time Deacon said, "It's her first time."

I glared. I glared hard and pictured his head exploding. How rude.

Katie flashed a wide grin my way. Her eyes lit up in excitement at having a total newbie in her hands.

"I'll take it easy on you," she said with a wink.

I did roll my eyes then, but she giggled, probably having taken it as playful.

Despite my misgivings, Katie turned out to be super

helpful and insightful. She knew which stands would give me the bigger push in my throws and how to throw it just right to have the axe spin a couple of times before hitting the target. She also introduced us to throwing knives. I liked those best. Unsurprisingly, it wasn't Deacon's first time with those either. *Show-off.*

After she was satisfied that we were comfortable with the axes and throwing knives and knew all the rules, she left us to ourselves with a promise that she would be close in case we needed her.

Deacon and I took turns in the cage trying different throws. I admit that after a while it started to become fun. In fact, I found myself relaxed enough to suggest a wager.

"What kind of wager?" Deacon asked skeptically.

"If you win, I'll wash your truck for a week."

He grinned, running a hand through his hair. "And if you win?"

His green eyes bored into mine, and I had to fight against the tidal wave that threatened to drown me. If I wasn't careful, I'd be trading one addiction for another. Deacon was an addiction on a whole new level, though. I wasn't sure if I'd be able to detox from him.

"If I win," I said, pretending to think about it. A slow smile pulled at the corners of my lips as I stared back at him. "You have to kiss me again."

"Leah," he breathed, like I was testing his patience and he was running out.

"Unless the next words out of your mouth are either in agreement or disagreement to the wager, then I don't want to hear it."

His jaw snapped shut as I cut him off and said my piece. I stepped up close to him — closer than I probably should have — and pressed a palm over his heart.

"Whatever you're telling yourself about that day, stop. I wanted it as much as you did."

"I don't want to push you or hurt you." His hands took my hips and pulled until my body was flush against his.

"You're not pushing me, and you're hurting me by denying us what we both want. I'm a grown adult, Deacon. I can make my own decisions, and I know when to say no if I can't handle anything or if things are going too far too fast." I pulled away only enough so that I could see his eyes and gulped. "Unless you don't trust me."

"I haven't known you long enough to not trust you."

I tilted my head to the side. "Don't people usually have to earn trust?"

"Not with me. I trust until someone proves they're not worthy."

"That's a very honourable way to look at it," I said and wrapped my arms around his waist, grinning cheesily on the inside when he returned the gesture.

"It's the way it should be. Unfortunately, I think the world has become jaded, and now the more common way is that someone must earn trust before they can break it."

He had a point. Nobody trusted easily today. It was sad, but after everything I had experienced before I was sixteen, it made sense.

"Enough of this heavy talk. Let's throw some axes."

Just as I stepped up for my turn in the cage, Deacon called out, "They have machetes in the back."

I froze and turned to him, thinking he must have been kidding. But nope. He stood with his hands in the pockets of his jeans and a smug look on his face.

"I'm sorry, what?"

He nodded toward a hallway against the same wall as the bathrooms. "Their rage rooms."

"What exactly is a rage room?"

His face lit up like a kid on Christmas. "They have tons of breakables you can choose from. Then you choose your weapon. They have a mix of machetes, axes, baseball bats, and some other stuff." He waved his hand in the air to indicate the "other stuff." "You pick your rage playlist, and then you go nuts."

Huh. That actually sounded… not bad. I would most definitely be interested in that. Maybe more so than the axe throwing.

"Hmm, maybe next time."

Surprise crossed Deacon's face before what I could only describe as pure joy took its place.

"Now, let's do this shit. I have a wager to win," I said and turned back to face the target at the other end of the cage. I chose a throwing knife this time. I had better accuracy with these fuckers anyway. Since I was up first, I had to make sure I got a bull's eye right off the bat. With Deacon's military training, I knew it wouldn't take any effort on his part to bulldoze me in this wager and win.

I stepped up the line and breathed in deep, holding it for a few seconds before slowly letting it out. I assumed the stance that Katie taught me, and following her instructions, I let the knife fly through my fingers. Then I did the worst thing you could do: I closed my eyes.

Chapter Sixteen

D eacon

I WATCHED AS THE THROWING KNIFE LEFT LEAH'S FINGERS and twisted through the air before coming to a stop in the middle of the red bull's eye. She opened her eyes and let out a loud whoop, drawing the attention of the other participants in nearby cages.

I didn't care. I would endure all the stares just to see her so happy and full of life. I still couldn't believe she'd called me on my shit, but I shouldn't have been surprised either. My sister did warn me that Leah was probably fiercely independent and as a result knew what she wanted.

My plan had been to go home and talk to her about what had happened at the cabin. I wanted to gauge where she was at.

That plan went to shit when I walked into the apartment and smelled that delicious smell and saw her standing in my kitchen. Images from that day flashed through my mind, and I had to bite my tongue until I tasted that metallic tang to stop myself from bending her over and having my way with her again.

A new image of Leah on her knees in front of me had my jeans tightening. I had to twist my hips slightly when she flew into my arms and hugged me so that she didn't feel the evidence of my attraction to her. I was sure she felt it anyway if the look she shot me was anything to go by.

"Your turn," she said smugly, and oh I wanted to kick her ass in this wager just to teach her a lesson.

The brief thought of winning this had crossed my mind, but the thought of getting to kiss her again won out. Although, having my truck washed every day for a month was appealing too.

It was a tough one. Leah shot me a grin and then sauntered out of the way so I could step into the cage. When she matched my gaze and slowly, deliberately licked her lips, I knew exactly what my decision would be.

My first throw hit the bull's eye, although not as close to centre as hers. Her next throw didn't even come close to the red circle in the middle, and because I couldn't make it seem obvious that I was going to throw the game, I threw mine to hit just outside of the red.

Leah pouted when she was up next, and it was the cutest thing I'd ever seen. God, the thought of biting that full bottom lip was almost too tempting. I think she had the right thought from the beginning.

We should've ditched this place and gone back home. At least there, I could walk around with the boner that was currently threatening to bust out from behind my zipper. I groaned and pressed the heel of my palm into the base of my cock.

Leah was up again, and this time, she hit the bull's eye again. She whooped, throwing her hands up in the air and giving her hips a little wiggle. We were coming up on the ten-minute warning of the end of our session. I just had to botch my next throw, and she would officially win the wager. When my knife barely made a dent in the very edge of the target before falling to the ground, I hung my head and stuck my hands in my pockets before turning back to her. Leah preened from where she stood just outside the cage.

The light from the overhead bulbs cast a yellow glow around her, making it look like a halo around her long, chocolate locks. The gold in her eyes sparkled, and her cheeks turned a pink hue when a blinding smile spread across her face. I had never met a woman more beautiful than her. None who were as genuine as she was either.

"I think our time's about up. Do you want to grab some appies here or go home, get into pajamas, and binge watch *Yellowstone*," I offered, but I already had a pretty good idea of which she would pick.

After only knowing her a little more than a week, it became apparent pretty fast that Leah wasn't a crowd person. Hell, I was almost positive she wasn't even a people person. The fact that she put up with my ass for a week in the middle of nowhere was a miracle in itself.

"Home," she said without hesitation.

We grabbed our jackets and headed back out into the night. The parking lot had cleared out a bit since we arrived, making the city more visible below the hill.

"Wow," Leah said, coming to a stop at the far end of the parking lot. "This is incredible."

"You should see it in the middle of winter when everyone still has their Christmas lights up."

She hummed and wrapped her arms around herself. I didn't even try to stop myself from stepping up behind her and folding mine on top of hers. My chin rested on her head.

"You know," she started, "everyone always says how they love going so far out of the city that the only thing you see are stars for miles. But I love this too. Looking at all the city lights. There's just something about it that I can't exactly explain."

"It makes you feel on top of the world, but also like a tiny part of it."

She tilted her head to the side to look up at me. "Exactly."

"There's this lookout that's a little higher up. You can see the entire city from up there. A real three-hundred-and-sixty-five view. It's one of my favourite places in the city. Maybe I'll take you up there sometime?" I meant it as a statement, but it came out sounding more like a question.

"I'd like that," Leah said, threading her fingers through mine and pulling my arms closer around her.

We stood there for a while, staring out over the small part of the city we could see. When more customers started spilling out of the axe throwing place, we headed for my truck and went home.

Chapter Seventeen

Leah

NERVES KNOTTED MY STOMACH WHEN WE STEPPED BACK into the apartment. Axe throwing had been fun, but I couldn't deny that I'd been looking forward to cashing in on my winnings ever since we'd gotten back in the truck and driven away.

Deacon hung his keys on the hook beside the door and toed off his shoes. I was on him the second he turned around. I reached up to grip the nape of his neck and pulled him down until I could get to his mouth. It had been way too long since I tasted him last, and I was starving. I wrapped both arms around his neck and greedily drank him down.

Ungh, fuck yes.

This. This was what I wanted.

He gripped my hips and picked me up, pressing my

back against the wall to bring us closer together. I moaned thankfully and wrapped my legs around his waist, rotating my hips when he settled between my legs.

We hadn't had penetrative sex yet, but I wanted it. Now. Today. I hoped he wouldn't stop it and make up an excuse again. I thought I was likely to scream if he did.

Deacon planted a hand on the wall beside my head and cupped my cheek with the other, slowing us down. We were both panting when we came up for air, and he pressed our foreheads together. I slowly opened my eyes and immediately felt like I was drowning in a sea of green. Every time I tried to surface to catch my breath, the rip currents pulled me back under.

"Deacon," I breathed, unsure of what I was asking for, only knowing that I needed him like the breath that filled my lungs.

He groaned. "When you say my name like that... fuck. I can't think." He nipped at my lips. My thighs tightened around him. "I want to give you everything."

My breath hitched at the admission. I framed his face with my palms and brought his face back up to mine from where it fell to my chest. "Just give me you. I don't need anything else."

His eyes blazed, and then he kissed me again, moving us from the wall and down the hall to his bedroom.

With me still clinging to him and an arm banded around my waist, Deacon planted a knee on the bed and then the other. He moved us higher up the bed before placing me down with such care that tears sprang to my eyes. I blinked them away and reached for him, my hands going for the buttons of his shirt.

His gaze never left mine as I tried to focus on steadying my fingers so I could unbutton his shirt and finally feel his skin on mine. I'd craved it since that day in the kitchen at the cabin.

Finally, the last button gave way. I pushed the shirt down his back and arms, and Deacon helped to tug it off from his wrists, tossing it on the floor beside the bed. My palms pressed to the warm skin of his chest. I licked my lips at the sight of the barbells in his nipples. It still shocked me that he had them pierced. Piercings were never something that attracted me before, but on Deacon, they were hot as fuck.

"Your turn," he rasped, sitting back on his knees so he could help me with my shirt.

I sat up and whipped the offending material off, then went in for another kiss. Like I'd predicted, I was addicted to Deacon's kiss, to the way he let me take charge at first, allowing me my exploration before he took over. And I surrendered without a fight. I had a feeling that I would always surrender to him, whether in the bedroom or out.

He laid us back down and settled more fully over me. My knees dropped open, making more room for him between my thighs. I could already feel him hard beneath his jeans, and I swallowed thickly at the anticipation thrumming through my veins as I traced lines down his torso to the tattoo on his hip and then to his waistband. Deacon sucked in a breath as my fingers hooked over the band and grazed his skin.

"Leah, is this —" His words cut off with a groan when I swiped my thumb over the head of his already leaking cock. "Is this what you want?"

I leaned up and nipped at his jaw, his earlobe. "So much," I whispered.

Deacon cursed. His jaw ticked as his nose flared, and then he was moving. He left the bed to grab condoms from the bedside table, and when he came back, he curled a hand around my ankle and yanked me to the foot of the bed. I squealed and then laughed. Fuck, that was hot. My pants were the next to the floor, with his joining them soon after.

I got a good look at Deacon completely naked. My tongue dried, and I couldn't swallow. Sweet mother of pearl. He was beautiful. His chest had a smattering of neatly trimmed black hair that tapered into a treasure trail down his belly. His cock was long, not too thick, and curved slightly to the left. I was speechless as my need to have him grew tenfold. I planted my feet on the edge of the bed and spread my legs wide as my fingers found my clit. I stroked it in a circle while I drew my gaze up and down his body.

Deacon gripped the base of his cock and squeezed, groaning. "If you keep that up, this is going to be over too fast."

"Then it's a good thing we have all night," I said, canting my hips up. "I'm so close already." I breathed his name then, just like I had out in the hallway.

That got him moving. He ripped open the condom and rolled it down his hard length, then dropped to his knees. His arms curled around my spread thighs and yanked me until I was teetering on the edge of the mattress. I shouted and removed my hand to curl them both in the sheets beside my hips as his tongue licked up my slit and then slid inside.

"Oh god," I panted.

My back arched off the bed as pleasure coursed through my body. I hadn't been lying. I'd already been close to coming, and if he kept that up, I was going to come way sooner than I wanted.

I wanted to hold off until he was inside me. I carded

fingers through his hair, curled them into a fist, and yanked until he was bent over me. Tasting myself on someone's lips was never something I cared for either, but the urge to taste myself on Deacon's tongue was like an inferno that I couldn't ignore. I reared up and captured his mouth, sinking my tongue between his parted lips.

Deacon groaned, hiking my thighs higher, and then he was right there. His lips never left mine as his cock pushed inside. I groaned into his mouth and pulled him closer, hating that even an inch separated us. My hips bucked in time with his thrusts, and I cried out when he shifted and hit that spot.

"Fuck." The word was guttural and strained. "You feel so damn good, Leah."

Sweat beaded along our bodies as we moved together. The tears I had blinked away earlier threatened to come back at the realization that, aside from the first time Deacon made me come on his tongue, this was the only time I'd truly wanted this.

For all intents and purposes, Deacon was my first, and as we both finished and came down from our highs, I knew I would cherish this night. Regardless of what came afterward.

Chapter Eighteen

Leah

I WAS PARALYZED WITH SUDDEN FEAR AS I STARED AT THE building in front of me. What had ever made me think I was ready for this? Because it sure didn't seem like I was. Fear of them looking at my resume, seeing the big gap in my employment history, and automatically knowing that I used to be an addict living on the street had my stomach doing backflips and cartwheels. I couldn't do this.

I turned and bumped into someone on the sidewalk. With a mumbled apology, I sidestepped them and headed back toward where Deacon was waiting in the car. I thought briefly about heading for the bus stop around the block instead, embarrassed that I couldn't even make it to the interview. Maybe I'd take the bus downtown and go find Mav and Skeet. Buy some down and forget about this idea that I could get and stay clean. That I could be one of those people who had jobs and a life outside of drugs. But I couldn't do that to Deacon and the thought of going through that withdrawal again was enough to propel me toward the truck.

I yanked open the passenger door of the truck and climbed inside. My hand shook as I reached out to close the door.

"Leah? You okay? What's wrong?"

"I can't do it." I let go of the tears I had been holding back. "They're going to take one look at me and laugh me away."

"What are you talking about?"

I held out my forearms. The marks may have faded some, but they were still there. Still obvious. A reminder of the mistakes I'd made. Ones that almost cost me my life. "They're not going to take me seriously. Not with these."

Deacon gently took both my wrists in his hands and stroked his thumbs over my pulse points. He was quiet for a moment, contemplative, before he spoke.

"These do not define you. They show how strong you are, how much you've overcome. Their opinions of you don't matter, Leah. You are so much more than these. Make them see that."

"How am I supposed to ignore their opinions if they're the ones hiring me? I can't live off you forever, Deacon. I need to do something to not feel —" I stopped and swallowed thickly.

"To not feel what?"

"Useless," I whispered. "Like a failure."

This had been a constant topic of contention for me. No matter how much progress I made in other areas, feeling useless because I didn't have a job or diploma had been ever present.

Tension rose in the car as I felt Deacon's anger rise. It was the same argument between us too. I knew he didn't think of me like that, but it was hard to make your brain see something from someone else's perspective when you'd spent so much of your life seeing it one way.

"Hey," he said and reached out to grip my chin. His voice was surprisingly gentle when I knew how frustrated he must be with me. "We've talked about this."

"I know." I blew out a breath. "It's just going to take me a while to rewire my brain."

The tension in Deacon's shoulders deflated at my confession. I knew he meant well and just wanted the best for me. He hadn't given up on trying to get me to go to counselling, but I needed more time. Then he said something that shocked me. Nobody, outside of my first foster mom, had ever asked me that before.

"How can I help you?"

I stared at him, mouth agape and probably looking like a guppy. *God, where to start?*

"Be patient with me," I blurted.

Deacon smiled, framed my face in his hands, and kissed me. "Always."

"And maybe hold my hand?" I gestured toward the building across the street.

He chuckled. "That I cannot do, unfortunately. Not this time."

He lined up our palms in my lap and intertwined our fingers. "You got this. I'll be right here the whole time. Breathe." He took a deep breath and held my stare as I mimicked his actions, then let it out slowly. I did the same. "Remember what Lilah told you?"

I grinned, remembering his sister's words. We'd

spoken on the phone almost every day since she randomly showed up at his apartment while he was at work. Several of those times she'd been on speaker while ~~Deacon hasn't been home~~. "I'm a badass bitch?"

[handwritten: talk about empowerment!]

~~Say it like~~ you mean it."

I blushed but did as he said. "I'm a badass bitch!"

He laughed. "There's my girl." Deacon leaned over and kissed me again, longer this time until I melted into him. "Now, go show them exactly why they should hire you."

My stomach tightened, and I somehow found the courage to let go of his hand and jump out of the truck again.

For the second time that day, I crossed over the street and made my way to the café. If this didn't work, I was going to drown my sorrows in a tub of cake batter ice cream and reruns of *One Tree Hill*, and I didn't care what Deacon said. Maybe I could convince Lilah to join me. Make it a girls' night.

With one last fortifying breath, I grabbed the handle and pulled open the glass door of the Dark Breeze café. Dark modern furniture greeted me as I stepped inside.

The dark, stained wood coffee bar took up most of the length of the place, with baristas bustling around on the other side of it. It was bright in there. Like, *really* bright. Almost as if the company wanted you to get your coffee and get out as fast as possible to make room for more customers. Only four bistro tables decorated the inside: two on each side.

The place was busy with the lunch crowd, and I felt awkward bypassing the line to get to the pickup counter. I tried valiantly to ignore the looks from the customers still in line, but it was hard when they felt like daggers. The barista manning the espresso machine looked annoyed as I tried to get her attention and asked for the manager.

She eyed me suspiciously, one blonde eyebrow rising toward her hairline. When it seemed she was sure I wasn't going to rob the place, she yelled over her shoulder toward the back door. Why she'd think I would be asking for the manager if I was going to rob the place was beyond me, but I shrugged it off.

A woman who couldn't be much older than my twenty-eight years of age pushed through the swinging door behind the bar. Her red hair was artfully done in loose waves around her shoulders, and the black romper she wore covered her legs down to her ankles while leaving her arms exposed and accentuated what few curves she had. When she approached the barista, who was now on to making her third, or maybe fourth drink since I had been standing here, the barista tipped her head in my direction.

Red glanced at me, the same expression crossing her face as the barista had.

"Can I help you?"

I shifted nervously from one foot to the other. The words Lilah said to me repeated like a mantra in my head as I stuck out my hand for her to shake. "My name's Leah Harris. I'm here for the interview."

Her hazel eyes did a slow perusal of me while she ignored my proffered hand. Not wanting to feel any more awkward than I already did in a crowded café, I withdrew my hand and bit my lip. If she had already found me lacking, it was cemented the moment she got a look at my bare arms. But unlike hers, the marks of my past were glaringly obvious.

"I'm sorry," she said in a bored voice. "The position has been filled." With a parting glance at the barista, who now had a knowing smirk on her face, she turned on her heel and went back through the door.

I curled a section of hair behind my ear and sighed while trying desperately to force back the tears that threatened to spill. I turned and was halfway to the door when a beautiful, raven-haired woman entered the café and sauntered up to the pickup counter.

"I'm here to interview for the barista position." I overheard her say.

I wondered if they'd give her the same attitude when they told her the position had already been filled, but to my surprise, the barista stopped what she was doing and motioned for the woman to round the counter. Together they went through the swinging back door.

"Don't take it personally," someone said to my right.

I turned toward a group of three women sitting at one of the bistro tables. Embarrassment bloomed across my cheeks at the realization that probably everyone in here had just witnessed that.

The woman who spoke stood up and held out her hand. "I'm Janelle." Her sandy-blonde hair was in a braid over her one shoulder, and square, oversized pink glasses sat on her pointed nose. Paint splatters adorned her denim overalls. Her green eyes looked kind, if not concerned, as I hesitated for a few seconds before reaching out and shaking her hand.

"Leah."

Her eyes shot down to the marks on my arm, but she quickly averted them back to my face. I wanted with bated breath for her and her friends to mock me about it, but she didn't even ask. Her friends didn't laugh or ask about them either.

"I run a bookstore a couple blocks away. Usually, I don't make it a habit of coming in here, but their coffee really is the best in town. Anyway, we couldn't help but overhear what happened. Are you okay?"

I glanced at the other two women still sitting at the table. They looked genuinely concerned too. I shrugged as I looked back at Janelle.

"Nothing I haven't experienced before."

"Well," one of the others said. She and Janelle looked alike from the matching hair and eye colour. But where Janelle looked like the artistic type, this woman was definitely more business casual in skinny jeans and a nice shirt topped with a black blazer. No glasses in sight. "We'll be finding a new café in town. I can't believe they'd do that when they've been desperate for more baristas for months."

The third woman snorted. "I can. They're a bunch of stuck-up snobs. Always have been. Working at a world-renowned café doesn't give anyone the right to be a bitch."

She jumped up from her seat and threw her arms around me. I was too stunned to hug her back, but it didn't seem like she minded when she pulled back.

"Hi. I'm Britt." Her blue hair was pulled into a ponytail high on her head, and the end swung back and forth as she practically bounced on her feet. She reminded me of a blue-haired Tigger.

"That's my sister, Anna." Janelle hitched a thumb over her shoulder to indicate the second woman. "Don't mind her. She's on a deadline."

"Hi," Anna said with a smile hidden behind her coffee cup.

"So, I know this is kinda weird since you've just met us and we sorta accosted you, but —" Janelle paused and pulled a card from the front pocket of her overalls. "If you're still looking for a job, I'd love to hire you," she said, handing me the card.

Clifton Books was sprawled across the top in fancy blue lettering against an off-white, almost sand-coloured background. The bookstore's address, phone number, and email were listed at the bottom.

"Um, thanks. I think?" I said, looking up from the card. "You don't know me, though. Why would you want to hire me?"

Janelle looked at Britt and then Anna, who nodded.

"Because," she said, turning her attention back to me. "We've all needed someone to give us a second chance. Plus, I think you may like working there better than here." She grinned, and it was so friendly that I couldn't help but return it.

"Well, I, um…" I paused to gather my thoughts and tried again. "Thank you," I whispered, feeling a bit overwhelmed at where this day had gone.

Britt squealed, drawing the attention of nearby customers, and pulled me into another hug. "I'm so excited you're going to be working with us. We'll have so much fun. We usually spend most of the shift reading and stocking shelves with the odd prank, but, well, you'll see!"

I wasn't even sure if she took a breath during all of that, but she must have because she didn't look or sound winded. She turned back to the table and grabbed her crossbody bag. "I'll catch you ladies later," she said, giving Anna a high-five across the table and pulling Janelle into a hug. Before I knew it, she was headed out the door and down the sidewalk, a pep in her step.

"She's, uh —" I didn't quite know how to finish that sentence without sounding like a judgemental ass to someone I just met.

Janelle and Anna laughed.

"She's Britt," Anna said when her laughter died down. "You'll get used to her."

"When should I come by the shop?" I asked Janelle, who had just taken a drink of her coffee.

"Are you free tomorrow? Wednesdays are usually pretty slow, so I'll have time to show you around, and you can get to know the girls a bit."

"That sounds great."

"Awesome. Come by around nine? I'll pick up coffee on my way." She glanced around the café with her nose wrinkled in disgust. "Not from here, though."

"Speaking of which," Anna said, packing up her stuff and standing to come around the table. She kept looking over our shoulders, so Janelle and I followed her gaze. The red-headed manager and the barista were staring at us with narrowed eyes.

"Welp," Janelle said, picking up her purse. "That's our cue to leave."

I followed the two sisters outside and onto the sidewalk.

"Thank you for this," I said, holding up the business card Janelle gave me before they could leave. I spotted Deacon's truck out of the corner of my eye. Knowing he was still in the same spot made me relax.

"Don't thank me yet. I'm just giving you the opportunity. It's up to you what you do with it," Janelle said, and then she and Anna walked over to a sedan parked in front of the neighbouring business and drove off.

Everything still felt so surreal when I got back in the truck and relayed all that had happened to Deacon while he drove us home.

"Sounds like you dodged a bullet," he said while we

waited for the elevator in the underground parking garage.

"Yeah. Maybe. They seemed nice anyway."

I got in the elevator first. When I turned around, I was momentarily surprised at how close Deacon was. I didn't even hear him hit the number for his floor. He backed me up until I was pressed against the mirrored wall. His one hand went to cup my cheek while the other gripped my hip.

"I'm proud of you."

I scoffed and tried to look away, but he didn't let me. "They didn't even give me a chance. They took one look at me and thought they knew me."

"Maybe," he said, leaning down until his breath ghosted my lips. "But you said they were going to. Even knowing that, you still went in there with your head held high." His seafoam-green eyes ping-ponged between mine, and a smile curled his lips. "Did you know you came out of there smiling?"

I frowned. "I did?"

"Whatever those women said to you, you weren't thinking about the manager and the barista. You looked happy."

I raised up on my toes and curled my arms around his neck, forcing his hand on my face to drop to my other hip. "You're right, I was. Those three women saw my scars and didn't judge me for them. Thank you for not letting me give up."

I closed the distance between our mouths and kissed him. I ran my tongue along the seam of his lips and licked inside. He tasted like the chocolate Tootsie Roll candies he kept in the glovebox of his truck. Deacon reached down and hooked his hand under my thighs, lifting me and causing me to wrap my legs around his waist. I moaned into the kiss and deepened it just as the elevator dinged and the doors slid open on our floor. I kissed and sucked down his neck as he walked us down the hall, leaning me back against the doorframe of the apartment while he fished out the keys.

He cursed when I undulated my hips and rubbed against him.

"Leah," he groaned, the hand still on my hip squeezing in an attempt to slow me down. "If you don't stop, we're going to give the security guys a show."

I caught the lobe of his ear between my teeth and gave it a good tug. "Then you better hurry."

"Motherfu —"

The keys rattled in the lock, and then he pushed it open and carried me inside. He paused only long enough to kick the door shut before carrying me down the hallway. We bypassed the guest room where I had been staying and went straight to the master bedroom.

Deacon deposited me on top of the covers, and I bounced a couple of times, never once taking my eyes off him. I still sometimes had a hard time believing he was mine.

He reached behind his neck and grabbed a fistful of his shirt before pulling it over his head and letting it drop to the floor. His jeans and briefs were next. I chewed on my bottom lip to stop the desperate moan. It was entirely unfair that he was gorgeously naked and I was still fully clothed.

"Aren't you forgetting something?" I asked.

He quirked a brow. His eyes blazed a trail down my body, and if I wasn't entirely certain that we were both mere mortals, I would've been sure that look alone would incinerate any clothing I'd been wearing.

"I didn't forget anything," he said, planting a knee on

the bed. "I plan to undress you very…" He planted the other knee and leaned over me. "Very slowly," he continued as he crawled up my body.

I squirmed, the material of my clothes suddenly feeling too scratchy and restricting against my skin. "Deacon."

His hands went to my hips and then slid up over my waist, dragging my top with it, but stopped just below my breasts. He met my eyes as his lips kissed a trail down my middle to my belly button. I shivered and watched in rapt fascination when he bit the waistband of my dress pants between his teeth and began dragging it over my hips. I planted my feet on the bed on either side of him and lifted my hips off the bed to help him.

Deacon growled around the fabric as, little by little, my underwear became exposed. He hadn't told me to keep my hands up, so when he'd gotten my pants below my ass, I hooked my fingers in my underwear and shoved them down.

He chuckled. "In a hurry?"

I swallowed. "No." It was obviously a lie, and his smirk said he knew that.

Either to spite me or drive me crazy, he took his time removing my pants and underwear from around my ankles. Deacon kissed the inside of one ankle and placed my foot back on the bed, then repeated it with the other. With each slow crawl back up my body, he placed a kiss on each of my calves, inner thighs, each side of my pelvic bone, and my belly.

"Are you trying to drive me crazy?" I asked, leaning up on my elbows.

He licked a stripe up the middle of my torso to my breasts. My shirt was still in the way. "That's the plan, yes."

I dropped back down with a groan. "Consider me adequately crazy," I said, then grabbed the back of his head and pulled him down for a kiss.

My shirt was the last to go, and then we were finally skin to skin. I wrapped my legs around his waist and canted my hips up. If my eyes weren't already closed, they would have rolled to the back of my skull when his hard length rubbed along my slit.

Deacon cursed and dropped his head to my shoulder. "Baby, if you keep doing that, I'm going to take you right now, and I need to grab a condom."

My hands slid down his back, tracing every curve until they reached his ass. I tried to pull him closer and whimpered when he pulled back.

"Please," I begged, desperate to feel him fill me again. We'd only had sex a couple of times before, and it had been several days since. I needed him to remind me how good it had felt, but somewhere in the back of my head, I also realized that I needed the validation. I wanted to feel good, yes, but I also wanted to know that he still found me desirable. That despite my past, he still wanted to make love to me.

Deacon sat back on his knees and reached over to pull a condom from the bedside table. I watched from under heavy lids as he tore the foil wrapper in two and rolled the condom down his dick. He bent over me again. I pushed my head further into the pillow and lifted my chin to meet his hungry stare.

Would I ever get used to this? I didn't think so.

I reached down and curled my fingers around the base of his shaft, giving it a hard stroke before aiming the head at my entrance. I was done playing games.

Apparently, that was all the encouragement he needed. Deacon braced his forearms on either side of my head and drove his hips forward, entering me in one thrust. I moaned and arched my back, my feet planted firmly on the mattress.

After our first time together — the cabin notwithstanding — I had decided that the next time we were in bed would be rougher. I knew there was a part of Deacon that needed that kind of raw passion. But it was like he knew the thoughts going through my head and that this type of slow, worshipping lovemaking was exactly what I needed right now. Maybe we could save the wild sex for later.

I hooked my arms under his and hugged him to me, needing to feel as much of his skin against mine as humanly possible. I felt needy and on edge, but Deacon didn't protest. He gave me exactly what I wanted, and like a tidal wave, my orgasm crashed over me with zero warning.

Chapter Nineteen

L eah

THE SAME CRIPPLING FEAR THAT HAD GRABBED HOLD OF me yesterday morning was back as I stood outside Clifton Books.

Logically, I knew that today wouldn't hold the same outcome as yesterday at the café. I'd already met Janelle. She'd already seen my scars and seemingly brushed it off. I had nothing to worry about.

Just get in there.

Still, there was a tiny voice at the back of my mind that cautioned me if something seemed too good to be true, it probably was. Maybe I'd watched too many teen dramas over the last few months while waiting for Deacon to get home from work. They made it seem like something like this always ended up being a prank or a bet. I couldn't bear it if it was. I didn't think I was mentally strong enough to overcome something like that on top of everything else.

"You have nothing to be nervous about," a voice said behind me.

I startled, a hand flying to my chest as I turned to see Anna.

She was wearing black dress shorts, a champagne-coloured cami under another black blazer, and cute black ballet flats on her feet. Her long, curly hair was up in a bun atop her head.

"Sorry," she said on a laugh. "I didn't mean to scare you."

"It's fine." I exhaled a loud breath and tried to get my heart to stop racing.

"Were you planning on coming in? Or just going to stand out here all day?"

"Honestly?" I asked.

She adjusted the strap of her purse higher on her shoulder and waited me out.

"I'm not sure."

A look of understanding crossed her face, and she smiled reassuringly. "Like I said before, you have nothing to worry about. Jannie isn't like those bitches at that café. But —" She moved closer until she was standing before me. "— if it'll make it easier, I'll wait and go in with you when you're ready. Then it won't seem so much like you're walking in there by yourself."

"You'd do that?" I asked, shocked.

"Yeah. Why not? We could go to the diner next door and get breakfast if you want."

Tears pooled in my eyes, but I swallowed them back. I needed to stop the waterworks and get my shit together. I hadn't cried this much since they told me my dad hadn't been sleeping.

"Okay," I croaked. "I'd like that."

"Cool. They make the best pancakes. I think you'll love it."

Anna looped her arm through mine and turned us in the direction of the diner. The breakfast rush had already started winding down by the time we made our way inside, so it was easy to grab a table by the big window overlooking the street and sidewalk. Anna chatted easily the entire time. The more she talked, the more relaxed I felt until it seemed like I was just talking with a friend I'd known for years.

True to her word, the pancakes were delicious, almost sinfully so, and I was stuffed after eating only two of the double chocolate chip and caramel stack I ordered — again, on Anna's recommendation — as well as the scrambled eggs and bacon it came with.

"I feel like I should be checking my blood sugars after that," I teased, wiping my mouth with a paper napkin.

Anna laughed. "Right?" She leaned against the vinyl backing of the booth and patted her flat stomach. "But so good, though."

She'd get no arguments here. Before Deacon, I hadn't had a meal like that in... well, it had been a while. The waitress came by and refilled our coffees, then collected our dirty dishes. We thanked her, and when she dropped the bill on the table, I hesitantly reached for it. I still had a little bit leftover from my last welfare cheque, but I had to be careful until I knew for certain that I had another paycheque coming in. Plus, I still wanted to put money away to give to Deacon. Even though he said he wouldn't accept payment for anything he'd done, I wouldn't feel right if I didn't at least try.

"I got it," Anna said, reaching for the bill at the same time.

I snatched it up before she could grab it and pulled my hand back. "It's okay. I can get it."

"Leah…"

"Anna, please," I pleaded and hoped that she could see everything I couldn't say reflected in my eyes. I needed to do this, and it was more than just paying for our breakfast.

She relented with a deep sigh, and my lips twitched. "Fiiine, but next one's on me." She smiled, and I couldn't help but return it.

"Deal."

My stomach swooped, and I had a moment of panic that maybe I wouldn't be able to afford it after all in the split second it took me to turn over the printed bill. I deflated in relief when I saw the total at the bottom. It wasn't as bad as I had thought. I mean, it wasn't great, but I could still treat Anna to breakfast and have a little something leftover.

We gathered our coats and made our way up to the till, where I paid for our meals. Just like earlier, Anna looped her arm through mine as we made our way out of the diner and back into the spring sun.

"Ready?" she asked, already steering us in the direction of the bookstore.

"As I'll ever be."

She giggled. "I promise, you'll enjoy it. And if you don't, then Jannie and I will find you something you will enjoy."

I stopped in the middle of the sidewalk, causing Anna to stop as well.

"Why?" I asked. "Why would you do that?"

For the first time this morning, her smile slipped, and I got a glimpse at the pain behind the sparkle in her eyes. "I'd guess that our stories aren't that different." She looked away, her eyes becoming unfocused for a minute or two before looking back at me. "Everyone deserves another chance."

"I, uh, I'm not ready to share my story."

Anna shrugged. "And I didn't ask you to. But just know that if or when you decide to, Jannie and I and Britt will be here to listen."

I didn't know these women from strangers on the street, but as soon as Anna said those words, I knew them to be true. I knew I could trust the three of them with whatever I had to say. I wasn't ready to share because I didn't know if they'd judge me. I wasn't ready to share because I didn't know if I was ready to relive a past that still felt too close.

I said the only thing I could think of in that moment. "Thank you."

"Of course." Anna beamed, then redoubled her efforts to guide me down the block to the bookstore.

Welp, here goes nothing.

Stepping through the front doors of Clifton Books was like stepping into another world. Six-foot-high shelves made of birch wood stood in rows down the far sides of the store. In one corner to the right of the front door and tucked away was a little reading nook with a bench seat under the window and a beanbag chair on the floor. A side table sat in the middle of them for readers to set their drinks or books down.

I followed Anna down the middle to the front desk, which was made of the same wood as the shelves. At the far back left corner beside the desk were long study tables that were being occupied by two students. To the right of the desk was a coffee station. It didn't look as fancy as the café did yesterday, but it had all the basics one would need to make a decent cup of coffee.

"Leah!" Janelle greeted me with a wide smile, rounding the desk between the coffee bar.

"Hi." I patted her back awkwardly as she enveloped me in a big hug.

She beamed as she pulled away, her perfect white teeth on display. "I'm so glad you made it! Let me show you around."

I glanced to Anna on my right. She giggled and with a wink took off toward the back of the store. Janelle spent the next few hours showing me around and getting me acquainted with how to stock the shelves and coffee bar. Thankfully, I wouldn't be tasked with making coffee. Everything over there looked so overwhelming I was afraid I'd screw up every drink order.

Books I could do. Books were easy. People didn't tend to lose their shit if a book they picked up wasn't quite to their tastes. But screw up someone's coffee? Might as well call in the National Guard. People took their coffee orders way too seriously.

After a while, Janelle had to leave me up front when her sister called her about a wedding emergency. The store had been fairly quiet all morning, so I felt confident I could handle things for a couple of hours while she dealt with whatever had come up.

Turned out, a couple of hours actually meant the rest of the day. When the clock on the computer ticked over into the two-hour mark, I started to get nervous. The store didn't get any busier, but there was a slow trickle of customers around lunchtime. When three hours passed, Anna poked her head out from the back office to see how I was doing.

"You didn't have to go deal with the emergency too?" I asked her.

Anna shook her head as she sorted through the new books that had come in. "We're not related. We call each other sisters because we've been friends for so long, but Chloe — that's Janelle's sister — and I never really got along."

At five hours, Britt stopped by the store and kept me company during a particularly long lull between customers. Anna joined us up front too. I was beginning to enjoy spending time with them, and for the first time in a long time, I thought maybe I could develop a friendship with these girls. I learned that Anna was a romance author. I had begged her to tell me the titles of her books and then promptly looked them up when she gave in. As soon as I could, I would buy one of them.

I smiled. It was a dumb thought, but I always felt disappointed that I'd missed out on sleepovers with my girlfriends and mall dates, gossiping about boys over milkshakes or whatever. What if I could have that with Janelle, Anna, and Britt? I hoped so.

Just as Anna had been showing me how to cash out at the end of the day and Britt was cleaning up around the store, the bell above the front door chimed as Janelle pushed it open. She looked flustered. Her once neat ponytail was loose, with wispy pieces of hair standing up around her face. Her eyes had lost some of its earlier joy. Frown lines creased her forehead, and there was a tightness to her lips that wasn't there before.

"I'm so sorry, Leah," she said, her chest rising and falling rapidly as she panted like she'd rushed all the way here. Maybe she had.

"It's fine. It was pretty slow for the most part. Anna and Britt kept me company and helped me out."

Janelle looked relieved at that. She smiled at Anna and let out a breath as Britt joined us and threw an arm around her shoulders.

"Everything okay with the wedding?" Anna asked, closing the cash drawer.

"Depends on your definition of okay."

Janelle looked exhausted as she moved to take a seat at the round table by the coffee bar. The three of us followed and took the remaining seats. The students from earlier had cleared out several hours ago.

"Richard's parents have now decided that they are coming to the wedding, so Chloe's freaking out. She wants to redo everything and make it fancier."

"Wait," Anna said. "Are these the same parents who refused to come to the engagement party because their son wasn't marrying someone of the same calibre?" Anna asked, adding quotations in the air around the last word.

"The very same," Janelle replied on a sigh. "She's losing her mind trying to get the best of everything so that Rich's parents will like her. The new florist she just hired?" She paused to meet each of our eyes. "Wants twenty grand for flower arrangements. That's not including bouquets for the bridal party."

Britt snorted. "Are these arrangements dipped in gold? What the fuck?"

I had to agree with Britt. Twenty grand for flowers that probably weren't going to last a day or two past the wedding seemed a bit excessive.

"You'd think so. The latest thing before I left were diamond chandeliers for the reception hall. I just... I couldn't hear any more. I mean, I know it's their big day, but she's digging herself into a financial hole she'll never be able to come out of. All for a man whose family doesn't give a shit about her." Janelle deflated even more as she spoke, and when she was done, her face crumbled as a tear spilled down her cheeks. "I love my sister, I do, but I don't know if I can watch her slowly lose herself to fit in with these people."

Britt pulled Janelle into a hug while Anna said, "Maybe it's time you talked with her."

She seemed to be the tell-it-like-it-is one, whereas Britt was the spontaneous one, and Janelle was the nurturer of the group.

I was in awe of how genuine their friendship seemed. Britt and Anna were ready to rally around Janelle and offered encouragement for her to have the difficult conversation with her sister. And there didn't seem to be any scores being kept. I was so used to the transactional relationship where everything was offered for a price that seeing this type of genuineness was mind-boggling but also beautiful in a way.

Not wanting to intrude any longer, I quietly pushed my chair back and stood. I gave them some lame excuse that I had to get back to the apartment, and after fielding their invitations to stay, I left the bookstore and began the ten-to-fifteen-minute walk back to Deacon's apartment, wondering if he'd be home already or if he'd had to stay later at work again tonight.

I missed him more than I was willing to admit to myself.

Yesterday, after we had gotten back, he'd gotten a call from one of his employees. There was an incident at one of the job sites that he needed to go deal with. He left and didn't come home until after ten at night. I had already been in bed after the anxiety of the failed job interview at the café and then meeting Janelle, Anna, and Britt, and then everything that happened in the truck. I'd been exhausted and promptly passed out in my bed after a quick dinner of Pizza Pops.

When I woke up that morning, Deacon had already left. There was a note on the kitchen counter apologizing that he couldn't take me to the bookstore but that he'd see me at dinner. Probably.

Although, I was pretty certain it was all in my head. It had only been a day; chances were good that he really had just been busy.

The fear that he would one day come back to the apartment and order me out was a constant niggle at the back of my head. If Deacon decided that he was done helping me and kicked me out, I'd be back to where I'd started with nothing. I couldn't let that happen. I didn't want to go back to being a homeless nobody. Not after I'd had a taste of what it was like to have someone care about if I've eaten or slept okay.

I stopped outside the door to the apartment and paused with the key halfway to the lock. I knew I needed to stop being fearful. I should just take Deacon at his word. He hadn't given me a reason not to trust him yet, and I was sure that if he were going to cut me loose, he wouldn't have gone through all the trouble of helping me get clean and putting a roof over my head and food in my belly.

"Stop being such a worrywart, Leah," I said to myself as I turned the key in the lock and pushed open the door.

The first thing I noticed upon entering the apartment was Deacon's work boots kicked off against the wall. So, he was home, then. The second thing I noticed, and almost a second too late before rounding the corner to the kitchen, was that Deacon wasn't alone.

My heart sank, and I swore at myself for the immediate reaction. It didn't necessarily mean anything.

Chapter Twenty

D eacon

By the time I got back to my place, I was exhausted from two days of dealing with a fuck-up from one of the suppliers. The rocks that had been delivered to the job site were nowhere near the ones the customer had wanted nor the ones I had ordered. We had already been running a couple of days behind schedule because they were late with delivery. When I got the text from one of my employees saying the rocks had arrived, I'd practically jackknifed out of bed, got dressed, and left for the job site within five minutes.

It had been a long day, but we managed to get the entire rock wall done. I was proud of the hustle and hard work my guys had put in today and as a result gave them the morning off tomorrow.

Tonight, I was looking forward to a quiet night at

home with Leah. Dinner, a few episodes of *MacGyver*, and maybe a repeat of yesterday.

There was a knock on my door, and as soon as I pulled it open to the person on the other side, I knew my hopes of a quiet night were dashed.

"What are you doing here?" I growled.

Her brown eyes flashed with something I didn't recognize before it was covered by sadness. She pulled her thin bottom lip between her teeth and blinked up at me, the same way she used to when she wanted something from me.

Back then, I'd fallen over trying to give her everything she could ask for. Now, I saw it for the lie that it was.

"Can I come in?" The melodious lilt of her voice still managed to wind itself around me like a comforting song.

Not wanting to give the neighbours any more to talk about, I moved to open the door wider for her to slip through. The moment I let her inside the apartment, I knew it was a mistake.

"Everything still looks the same," Chloe mused as she walked around the living room, running her fingers along the bookshelves we spent picking out one weekend from an antique sale.

I sighed, pinching the bridge of my nose. I didn't have enough energy to deal with whatever bullshit brought her to my doorstep. "What do you want, Chloe?"

She stopped in front of the sliding door that led to the balcony. The setting evening sun cast a halo around her, making her look almost angelic as she turned to face me.

"I'm getting married."

I sucked in a breath, expecting to feel the telltale ache in my chest, but it wasn't there. Despite the way our relationship ended, things hadn't always been that bad. That toxic. I liked to believe that we both loved each other in the beginning. Some of the things we shared… nobody could fake that.

"Congratulations," I said, walking around the island that separated the kitchen from the living room, and opened the fridge to grab a water. I grabbed another one and offered it to her.

"Thanks."

"I'm happy for you, Chlo, but what does that have to do with why you're here?"

She eyed me as she placed the plastic bottle on the counter and walked around it until we were toe to toe. Her palm pressed against my chest, warm and familiar, as her scent of roses and vanilla swirled around me.

"I was hoping," she purred as her hand ran down my front to the hem of my dirty T-shirt, "that we could have one last night. A final goodbye of sorts."

Her fingers grazed the waistband of my pants, her warm fingers sliding along my skin. I gripped her wrist in my hand to stop her before she could slip her hand down my pants.

"I thought you said you're getting married."

She lifted on her tiptoes. Her lips moved against my jaw. "I miss you, Deacon."

"Chloe," I warned and took a step back, eyes glancing at the clock. Leah was going to be home soon from her first day at work.

Chloe followed me back, uncaring about the distance I'd been trying to put between us. I wondered if her fiancé knew that she was here.

"Come on, Deacon. I know you want one last night too."

I shook my head and slid to the side and out of touching distance. "We've been over for a long time, Chloe. I've moved on. You should too. Go home to your fiancé," I said, hoping she'd get the message and leave before Leah got home.

Just as I had that thought, two things happened at once. One, Chloe definitely did not get the message and stepped close to me again, and two, the front door opened, and Leah appeared around the corner. Her eyes bulged wide at another woman in the apartment.

At Leah's gasp, Chloe turned a look over her shoulder. Her shock was visible on her face, but it was short-lived. The shock quickly morphed into a look I had seen a time or two while we had been together. Chloe was a shark, and she smelled blood.

Leah looked ready to bolt, and I couldn't blame her. I slipped around Chloe again and went to her, curling an arm around her shoulders and drawing her into a hug, effectively cutting off the stare down Chloe had initiated.

"How was your first day?" I asked, dropping a kiss to her forehead. I didn't know what possessed me to do it, but it felt right.

"It was good," she answered, her eyes still trained on Chloe.

I was prepared for Leah to make up an excuse to either hightail it back out of the apartment or head down to the room. It had stopped being her room the minute we slept together. So it shocked the hell out of me when she stepped out from under my arm and introduced herself to my ex with an outstretched hand.

"Hi, I'm Leah. Deacon's... roommate."

She was a hell of a lot more than that, at least to me, but I didn't correct her. I would later come to regret that I hadn't.

Chloe raised a brow and glanced down at Leah's proffered hand like she was afraid she'd catch something contagious. Her lips thinned until they disappeared, and she stared at Leah with a look of contempt that eventually made Leah withdraw her hand and shuffle awkwardly on her feet. I wanted to shake Chloe and ask what the hell was wrong with her, but I already knew the answer. She saw everyone who wasn't as rich as her as beneath her. Which amused me because that group included her family. Chloe amassed her fortune after she entered the workforce. Her parents and her sister weren't part of the group she associated herself with nowadays.

Leah seemed to shrug it off well enough, which was a change from the uncertainty she'd arrived at the apartment with when she saw Chloe. I stepped up behind Leah in quiet reassurance. I knew she wasn't stupid. The brief look she gave me when she got home told me she knew who Chloe was, I assumed thanks to my sister since Leah and I hadn't exactly had the ex conversation. I gripped her hip in my hand and subtly pulled her until her back was pressed up against my chest. The physical contact was more a reassurance for me that she was here than anything. It didn't help that ever since yesterday, whenever she was in close proximity, I had to touch her.

I had this insane need to kiss her again. To feel her lips move against mine. Her breath on my skin. I felt Chloe's stare bore into us from across the room. When I looked up, her expression twisted in shock, her mouth agape, but she recovered quickly.

"Well," she said, gathering her purse from the counter, "this has been an interesting day, but I must get going." She moved around the counter and came to a stop beside me. She paused, obviously waiting expectantly for me to offer to walk her out, but I wasn't about to do that. With a quiet huff, she said, "It was nice seeing you again, D."

Chloe didn't spare Leah a glance before she turned, stepped into her heels by the front door, and left.

Leah turned around to face me, hooked a hand around my neck, and pulled me down for a kiss. I groaned into her mouth and pulled her closer by her hips. I couldn't get enough of this woman.

She pulled away after too short a time. I followed her lips, wanting to close the distance again. She giggled, rubbing a hand down my chest, and stopped me from closing the gap.

"Something to remind you who you belong to. I'm going to change. You up for a couple episodes of *MacGyver*?"

"I was just about to cue it up when Chloe showed up. How do you feel about pizza and cheese bread for dinner?"

She grinned, her eyes shining brighter than I'd seen them since meeting her in that alley.

I held her close and nuzzled her neck.

"That sounds amazing. I'll be right back," she added, then slipped around me and headed down the hall to the guest bedroom.

WE DIDN'T GET MUCH FURTHER THAN HALFWAY INTO THE second episode of our binge-watching marathon, the rest of the pizza forgotten, when Leah turned in my arms and straddled my thighs.

I gripped her hips, assisting her as she moved back and forth over my dick. I pushed my head into the pillow and lifted my hips, pressing harder against her heat on a deep groan.

"Fuck."

Leah panted, her fingers curling into the T-shirt that covered my chest as she rode me through our clothes. She moaned, her movements speeding up as her orgasm got closer. I hooked a hand around her neck and pulled her down, smothering her lips with mine as she came. I followed right behind her and spilled inside my sweatpants like a fucking teenager.

We both breathed heavily as she lay down with her head on my chest. I knew I'd have to get up and sort out the mess in my pants, but for now, all I wanted was this. I curled an arm around her back and traced patterns into her shoulder.

About another episode into the show, I suddenly remembered my mom's request from the other day and cursed.

"What is it?" Leah asked, turning to rest her chin on my chest as she looked up at me.

"My mom invited us to Sunday brunch this weekend."

She laughed. "And you thought now was the best time to bring it up?"

I shrugged apologetically. "I'd forgotten until just now. You kinda short-circuited my brain." I grinned when she shook her head on a laugh. I'd truly never get tired of that sound. "So, you'll come?"

She sighed and settled her back down to watch the TV. "I guess we can't keep putting off their invitations forever."

I knew she didn't mean it as the chore she made it

sound like. Leah's own experience with family wasn't the greatest, so I didn't take it personally. I just hoped that after brunch with my family, she realized that no two families were the same. Mine was nothing like the foster ones she was sent to as a child. My family would rather die trying to protect her, a practical stranger, than hurt you.

I dropped the subject after that, and after a quick break to clean myself up, we cuddled back on the couch for a *John Wick* marathon.

Chapter Twenty-One

L eah

Deacon pulled into the driveway of a beautiful Spanish-style house at the edge of town. A mix of pink, peach, yellow, and white roses were in full bloom up the side of the driveway and along the front of the walkway that led to the house. Big, open windows lent to natural sunlight that streamed through the home. I could see several people already inside. I pulled and twisted the hairband around my wrist, my nerves getting the best of me before we were even inside.

"Hey," Deacon said, placing his hand over mine and halting the nervous tic. "It's going to be okay."

I shook my head and sank my teeth into my bottom lip as my eyes snapped over to the main window above the flower bed. "How do you know that? What if they don't like me? I don't exactly have the best past."

I lowered my eyes from the smiles and silent laughter on display. I had been doing better with my feelings of not belonging, but seeing where Deacon grew up twisted something in my gut. What if these people thought I wasn't good enough to date their son or brother? What if when they looked at me all they saw was the homeless junkie I used to be?

"They'll love you." Deacon reached out and hooked a finger under my chin, forcing my face up to his. "Plus, you've already met Lilah."

I swallowed hard. That was true. It meant it was one less new person I'd have to meet today. But… "You can't possibly know that, Deac —"

"That's just it. I do know." He twisted so he could face me more fully and took my face between his hands. "They'll love you because I do."

I blinked through the tears that I wasn't even aware had fallen until that very moment. "What?" I breathed.

His thumbs caressed over my cheeks, wiping away the tears. His eyes were brighter like the clearest waters of the Mediterranean when he smiled.

"I know it hasn't been that long, and the way we met wasn't conventional by any means," he chuckled, and I laughed in agreement, "but I think I've been in love with you for a while."

I sucked in a breath and clasped his wrists. "I was afraid I was the only one feeling this way."

In a move that was so quick I barely had time to register it, Deacon undid my seat belt and hauled me into his lap. He kissed me with all the passion I'd seen burning behind his eyes when he told me he loved me. We were both panting when we pulled apart, and his hands cupped my neck, his thumb stroking along my jaw.

"Definitely not the only one," he rasped. His eyes bounced between my lips and my stare.

I curled my fingers around the back of his neck and leaned down to kiss him again.

"Do we still have to go in there?" I asked, resting my forehead against his.

He laughed. "Only for a few hours. Then we can go home and spend the rest of the day in bed."

I moaned and circled my hips. He was already starting to harden, and I wondered if I had time to make him come before anyone noticed we were out here. But just then, someone hollered from the front door.

"Get a room!"

I glanced over my shoulder toward the front of the house and spotted a group of who I assumed were Deacon's siblings watching us with matching grins.

Deacon groaned, dropping his head back against the seat. "I'm going to kill them," he grumbled. "They're dead to me."

I grinned, the nervousness from earlier absent for the moment. "Hmm," I hummed, "I don't think orange is your colour."

He raised a brow as his head lifted from the seat. "Oh, just you wait," he teased with a nip to my earlobe. I shivered and then giggled as he tickled my sides. I tried squirming away, but there wasn't anywhere to go seeing as how I was straddling him in the driver's seat.

"Alright, alright," I wheezed. "We should probably get out there before they come over here."

"Yeah," Deacon sighed. "You're right."

We got out of the vehicle. Deacon took my hand before setting the alarm on the truck and leading me up the pathway to where most of his siblings still stood at the door.

"Don't crowd the poor girl," a voice said from behind everyone. They all parted, and a beautiful older woman stepped forward. Her dirty-blonde hair was swept up into a high ponytail, and her hazel eyes shone as they took in our clasped hands. "Drake, Dash, go help your father set the table," she spoke without having to look behind her.

Two men who looked younger than Deacon broke away and slipped back inside the house.

"You must be Leah." She beamed at me. Laugh lines appeared around her eyes.

"Mrs. Rutherford," I said in greeting, holding out my hand. Some of the nerves I felt in the car were back.

Deacon's mother waved me off and then pulled me into her arms for a hug while saying, "Please, call me Diana." She pulled away just enough to see my face but kept her hands on my shoulders. "You are even more beautiful than I imagined."

I blushed. An awkward smile pulled at my lips as I said, "Thank you." I didn't think I'd ever get used to being called beautiful or pretty.

"What am I? Chopped liver?" Deacon teased, and I was never more grateful to him for taking the attention off me for a moment so that I could catch my breath.

"You are beautiful too, son," his mother said, a teasing grin on her face as she pulled him into a hug next. His remaining siblings snickered. "Okay, enough of letting the cold air out. I'm not cooling the whole neighbourhood. Everyone inside."

Deacon shook his head on a laugh, and we followed everyone inside. Just as I imagined from seeing the outside, the inside was just as beautiful. The ceilings were high, with wooden beams running across. There was a staircase to the right that led up to the second-floor landing. A railing on the second floor ran the entire length of the entryway, allowing anyone upstairs to look over and see who had entered the house. Just beyond the entranceway was a door that stood slightly ajar. From the little I could see inside, it looked like an office. The door beside it was closed.

Across the hallway was a formal dining room, and at the back of the house were the large open-concept family room and kitchen. The entire back wall of the house was floor-to ceiling windows that looked out at a gorgeous backyard. The entire house was something out of a dream.

Lilah ran up to us as soon as we stepped foot into the family room. She wasn't part of the group that met us at the front door. The blue summer dress swirled around her thighs as she came to a stop in front of us. Her dirty-blonde hair was piled high on her head in a cute bun.

"D!" she squealed, throwing her arms around Deacon.

An oomph left him as he was pushed back by the collision, but he managed to catch her and himself from falling backward.

He laughed. "Hi, baby girl."

"I missed you," she managed between sniffles.

"We saw you the other week," another of Deacon's siblings said from the couch.

Lilah stepped out of Deacon's arms and shot a death glare over her shoulder at her other brother. "Your point? I can still miss him, Dashell."

Dash lifted his hands, palms out in surrender.

"Leah!"

"Hi." I lifted my hand in a weird, awkward wave thing and then promptly dropped it. She was the second person in the span of minutes who pulled me into a hug.

I side-eyed Deacon, who just shrugged, a sly smile curving his sexy mouth.

"D didn't tell you we're a huggy family, did he?" Delilah asked. She must have caught the look I sent her brother.

"No," I said, "he didn't." We'd only hung out a couple of times since the first time we met, but she hadn't hugged me then. I'd assumed because Deacon had told her about my aversion to touch, especially from people I didn't know.

"I'm sorry. If —" Diana started to say.

I shook my head and cut her off. "No, it's fine. I just…" I trailed off, not sure how much he'd told the rest of his family about me, but then decided to say fuck it. I'd never hidden who I was or where I came from, and I wasn't about to start now. Even if the thought of Deacon's family finding out about how we met had my stomach twisting. "I'm not used to it, but it's fine, really," I added. "It's… nice."

Diana still looked unsure, but she must have decided to take me at my word because she sent me a small smile and then continued moving about the kitchen.

His sister turned the full effect of her smile on me, then slipped her arm through mine and pulled me away from Deacon after asking if I'd already met the rest of the family. She pulled me to the couch and pointed to each person respectfully as she introduced me to the rest of their siblings and their dad, Michael. Damien, Dash, Drake, and Donovan were the other brothers.

Deacon and two of his brothers were the spitting image of their dad. All four had dark, rich black hair and piercing seafoam-green eyes. His other two siblings took after their mother — dirty-blond hair and hazel eyes. The entire family was beautiful.

Lilah and I sank into an easy conversation about her twins and the degree that she'd just finished. I'd only known this woman for a couple of months, and I was already in awe of her.

I didn't think I was capable of raising two kids while going to school. Hell, I didn't even possess the capacity to work full-time right now. And the thought of being stuck in one place for eight hours sent an overwhelming surge of anxiety through me.

Deacon had told me multiple times that I didn't need to dive headfirst right away. I could start off with one or two shifts a week and then work up to full-time if that's what I wanted. I think he mostly said that because he was afraid I might relapse if I tried to take on too much at once, which was fair. I knew the rate of relapse was high in the first several months, but I was committed to this. I didn't want to go back to living on the streets and being dependent on a drug that could just as easily take my life.

A part of me felt guilty for not reaching out to Mav and Skeet since that first text I sent after we got back from the cabin. Honestly, I didn't think I was strong enough yet for my two worlds to collide. If I was going to be successful at staying clean and getting my life back on track, I needed to keep my past separate.

Deacon and his brothers had stepped outside into the backyard but came back in when Diana announced that brunch was ready. He pulled out a seat for me at the table, and I was halfway to sitting when Diana asked me if I'd like a mimosa too. I felt more than saw Deacon freeze at her offer of alcohol.

"Mom," he chastised.

Diana sent a confused look at her son, and I could see the moment she realized her mistake. It was like it happened in slow motion. Her eyes went wide, and a blush of embarrassment crept along her cheeks as she stammered out an apology.

"I'm so sorry. I wasn't thinking."

"It's fine, really," I said. I guessed that answered my question about how much Deacon had told his family about me. Everything, apparently. Surprisingly, I wasn't mad about it. I actually felt relieved. "I can't expect anyone to stop doing what they enjoy because of me." I looked up at Deacon and placed a hand over his. "I'm okay. I promise."

He looked unsure for a moment, like he was getting ready to argue but then thought better of it. It was true. Just because I was recovering from an addiction didn't mean that everyone around me had to stop drinking. Alcohol was never my vice anyway. I tended to steer toward the harder drugs like heroin.

Diana still looked unsure, and I was racking my brain trying to come up with something that would make her feel better. Turned out, I didn't have to because Lilah had it handled.

"Mom, she said it was okay. I'm sure if it wasn't, Leah would've said so."

I sent her a grateful smile across the table, and she winked in response. Diana seemed to relax at that and settled into her seat to the right of Michael.

Despite that awkwardness, brunch went well. Everyone delved into easy conversation, and Deacon's family made a point to include me, for which I was thankful.

Even still, I enjoyed sitting back and watching them all tease and roast each other while telling embarrassing stories. I couldn't help but imagine that this was what a family should look like.

Deacon and I left a couple of hours later after helping his parents clean up the kitchen. Lilah made me promise that I'd have coffee with her this week, and I couldn't say no. I loved her energy and how she didn't bullshit. She called it like she saw it and was unapologetic about it.

I needed more of that confidence in my life. I hoped that it would eventually rub off on me. She had told me that she saw us being good friends the very first time we hugged goodbye, so there's that.

When we got home, I made a beeline for the bathroom and started to get the tub ready for a bath. It was still early in the day, not quite two o'clock, but I needed the downtime to process everything that happened.

I'd just stripped off the last of my clothes when the door opened and Deacon stepped into the room.

"Do you want to be alone?" he asked, his hands stuffed into the pockets of his jeans and shoulders hunched.

I kicked my underwear off and stepped closer to him. I took the hem of his shirt and lifted it off, dropping it to join the pile of my clothes on the tile. "No."

Deacon waited patiently as I slowly undressed him. I kissed each expanse of skin I uncovered. By the time he was as naked as I was, there wasn't an inch of skin I hadn't pressed my lips to. He silently vibrated with need, jaw clenched as he let me take the lead. I slipped my palm against his, taking his hand and towing him toward the tub. I waited as he got in first and scooted to the edge to make room for me in front of him.

The water splashed as I shifted until I was reclined with my back pressed to his front. Deacon cupped his hand under the water and brought it up to my chest. We watched as it ran a trail down between my breasts before disappearing beneath the wealth of bubbles.

I sighed, dropping my head back against his shoulder, and felt my body let go of all the stress I'd been carrying for months.

Today didn't go as expected, which was a good thing. His family practically welcomed me with open arms, and aside from that little hiccup with his mom, which wasn't really a hiccup in my eyes, they hadn't brought up anything about my past. Not in a negative sense anyway.

I thought that maybe I could see myself fitting in easily with his family. Lilah and I were already on our way to being fast friends. I'd never had close female friends, so the fact that I'd gained four was a huge deal. I hoped I didn't screw it up or that they grew tired of my baggage. I had a lot of baggage. I briefly wondered if they'd all be up for a girls' night one night this week.

Deacon's hands began wandering over my body. One palm cupped my breast while the other trailed between my legs. I gasped and moaned as my legs fell open as far as they could, given the size of the tub, and all thoughts of planning a girls' night evaporated.

Chapter Twenty-Two

Deacon

I groaned and cursed, gripping her waist tight in one hand as I used my other to keep from crushing her under my weight as her inner walls pulsed around my dick. Leah loosened the almost death-like grip her arms had around me. I sat back on my knees, took her hips in hand, and shifted her until I had the angle I was looking for.

She moaned and arched her back, driving herself down my shaft. I couldn't hold back any longer; I pounded into her. Sweat beaded and dripped off my forehead to land between her breasts.

My balls drew up tight, and I knew I wasn't going to last long. I took her hips in my hands and rolled us until I was on my back, and she straddled me, my cock still lodged deep inside her.

Leah giggled and pushed a strand of hair that had gotten loose behind her ear. God, I loved that sound. It was just as good, if not better, than the sound of her moaning my name as she came.

I planted my heels on the bed and drove up into her, feeling the telltale sign of my fast-approaching release. Even though she'd just come, Leah rode me like a fucking champion. I swore and thrust up into her once more, straining as my cum filled the condom.

She shivered, and then despite us both being a sweaty mess, she lay on top of me, keeping me inside her. Her head rose and fell with each ragged breath I drew in, but she didn't seem to mind.

"I need to take care of the condom," I said, trailing fingers up and down her slick back.

She hummed but made no move to let me up. "In a minute."

I wound my arms around her and held her. Obviously, she needed it, and who was I to deny her?

Several minutes passed before she moved to lie on the bed beside me, and I got up to take care of the condom. When I came back, I turned out the lights, then climbed into bed beside her and pulled her into me until her back was pressed up against my front. She wiggled her butt against me with a sigh and linked our fingers together over her belly.

"Despite how it started, I think today was a good day," she said.

"I'm glad."

We lapsed into a comfortable silence, and I was halfway to sleep when her voice cut through the silence.

"I think I'm ready to see someone."

"Yeah?" I asked, trying not to sound hopeful.

I had been hoping she'd come to this conclusion on

her own. Therapy could be the difference between someone relapsing or being successful in their sobriety.

"I at least want to give it a chance. I think it's time."

I squeezed her briefly and kissed her head. "I'll be here every step of the way."

Leah started wiggling out of my arms, so I let her go. She turned around and nudged me onto my back, then cuddled into my side with her hand over my heart.

"Thank you," she murmured as her breaths evened out, and she fell asleep.

THE NEXT MORNING, MY SISTER POUNDED ON THE DOOR just as I was getting things ready to make breakfast, and Leah emerged fully dressed from the bedroom.

"Oh, good. You're awake," Lilah said with a grin when I opened the door.

"Unfortunately," Leah muttered behind me on her way to the kitchen.

I laughed. My girl was definitely not a morning person.

"And you're dressed!" Lilah chirped, bouncing into the kitchen. She made herself at home, grabbing a travel mug from a cupboard and fixing herself some coffee before going for Leah. My sister placed the travel mug in one of Leah's hands and grabbed the other.

Ahh, that makes more sense. Lilah hadn't drunk an ounce of coffee in years, so I was confused as to why she'd started now.

"Hey! What the hell, Delilah?" Leah protested. With a look of horror on her face, she looked back toward me. My sister ignored her and continued to drag her out of the apartment.

"We're going for breakfast. Later, big bro," Lilah said, and then the door slammed closed behind them.

I stood in shock, staring at my front door for another minute or two, trying to comprehend what the hell just happened. But it was Lilah — there would be no explanation that would make sense. After another beat or two, I pulled out my phone and sent off a group text to my brothers, asking if they wanted to meet at the Apple Bowl field to play a quick game. I had the afternoon off, and it'd been a while since I'd seen my brothers.

The responses filed in almost immediately. Everyone agreed to meet around one o'clock. Including Damien.

Van was already there, leaned up against the side of his car, when I pulled into the parking lot, so I parked beside his Charger. It seemed no one had arrived yet. I groaned and pushed my head back against the seat for a brief second before getting out of the truck and joining him. I'd been avoiding this conversation for a while, but it looked like that was no longer an option.

"Hey. How's it going?" he asked, clapping a hand on my back when I pulled him into a hug.

"Can't really complain." I tossed the football between my hands, and I took up a spot beside him. "How've you been?"

He slid his hands in the pockets of his blue joggers and crossed an ankle over the other. He stared down at the gravel of the parking lot as he answered. "Work's been busy." He sighed and shook his head. "Ryan left."

"Shit." Van and Ryan had been together for going on twelve years. They'd met during Van's sophomore year of college and hit it off right away. They'd moved in together after Van graduated and were talking about buying a house this year and maybe starting a family.

"When?"

"Few days ago."

I cursed. "Jesus, Van. I'm sorry."

He pushed away from the car and kicked a piece of debris with his foot. "Not your fault."

I was about to ask him how he was holding up, but a line of cars pulled into the parking lot and parked up beside us. The rest of our brothers joined us.

"We going to play ball or what?" Drake hollered as he rounded the back of his truck and joined Van and me. Damien and Dash were behind him.

I glanced at Van, wondering if he was going to tell the others, but he gave a quick shake of his head and then headed toward the field. Drake and Dash followed him.

"He okay?" Damien asked as he caught up with me.

Dash pulled threw an arm around Drake's neck and pulled him in for a noogie while Damien and I trailed behind the three.

"Ryan left a few days ago," I said when I was confident the gossips of our group were far enough away to not hear.

"Fuck," Damien said.

"Yup."

"He say why?"

We reached the entrance to the field but held back while the other three argued about how we were going to separate into teams since there were an odd number of us. There was only one way to solve this if we had any hope of actually playing a game today instead of watching the three stooges argue all day. I pulled out my phone and sent a quick text, pocketing it again after the reply came through.

"No," I said, answering Damien. "I don't think he's ready to talk about it."

"I'll kill him if he hurt Van."

"I'll be right there with you, brother."

A few minutes later, our dad walked onto the field. He was nearly pushing sixty, but the man could still move like someone half his age. The man played football right through college and then went on to coach while attending law school. He'd never missed a workout either, except for the day Lilah was born.

We split into two groups — Dad, me, and Drake on one team and Damien, Van, and Dash on the other. Dad tossed a coin to see who would be losing their shirts. I breathed a sigh of relief when it landed on heads, meaning that Damien's team would be shirtless for the duration of the game.

I'd come a long way in my fitness journey since starting my rock wall company, but I wasn't where I wanted to be yet. I was getting there, though. Soon, the weight I had put on during my relationship with Chloe and subsequent dive into depression would be gone.

Dad took on the role of quarterback for our team since his throwing arm was ten times better than Drake's or mine. The game started out as a friendly touch-football game between family, but soon our competitor sides came out, and it quickly turned into full tackle. Dad threw the ball downfield to me on the next play.

I jumped and caught it, cradling it close as I landed and spun toward the end zone. A flash of movement to my right caught my eye, and I barely managed to brace as Dash barrelled into me, knocking me on my ass. I tried to maintain my hold on the ball, but as soon as my back hit the grass and my breath whooshed out of me, it tumbled out of my fingers.

"Fuck, man. You okay?" Dash asked, holding out a hand to help me up.

I remained on the ground as I wheezed and coughed, trying to catch my breath. Fuck me, that hurt like a motherfucker.

"I think you broke him," another of my brothers mused.

"Fuck off," I rasped.

That made them all chuckle. I sat up with a groan and accepted Dash's hand up. I needed another minute before I'd be good to go again. I made my way over to the bleachers and sat down for a beat, taking a drink from the water bottle I'd been smart enough to bring this time.

Dad and Damien joined me after a bit. We sat and watched the younger guys fool around on the field.

"Your mom wants to know if you'll be at the fundraising dinner next week," Dad said, wiping his forehead with a workout towel. It had been hotter than expected today, with a high of close to thirty degrees Celsius.

I waited to see if Damien would respond first, but he remained silent. Bastard. I knew he was waiting me out too. Waiting to see if I would break first. We usually took turns with these sorts of things. I'd lost track of which one of us attended the last one, though.

"I already told her I would," I admitted. Mom had cornered me during the last Sunday family brunch until I agreed to go. I had hoped I could just pawn it off on Damien, but I guessed that idea was out.

Dad hummed in approval, then asked if I was bringing Leah. I gave him a noncommittal answer. I hadn't decided if I was going to ask her or not. Not because I didn't want her there, but because she'd just started dealing with some of the things from her past. I didn't want to pick at an open wound by making her sit through this dinner.

The other three joined us again. Van and Drake said they needed to end out as they were both called in to work. We all said goodbye out in the parking lot by the cars, and I made a mental note to invite Van out for beers and wings one night.

Damien stayed behind as the others left. I scowled at him.

"You did that on purpose."

He snorted in amusement. "Prove it."

"Bastard," I huffed.

We fell into an easy silence then, both of us staring off into the distance. I had to get going soon, but I sensed that Damien had something on his mind, so I waited.

And waited.

After several long minutes, he cupped a hand behind his neck and tilted his face upward. "I got an invite from Wheeler."

I froze. "Did you accept?"

He shook his head, dropping his hand. "No. Don't know if I will. It's… been a while."

"I thought you were done with that lifestyle?" I asked.

"I was, but —"

"But it's them," I finished for him.

"I just wanted you to know. In case I end up leaving for a few days."

I nodded. Whenever Wheeler was involved, Damien went MIA for at least a week. Sometimes longer depending on his recovery period. I didn't know much about the BDSM lifestyle, but if it helped my brother navigate through the darkness that had settled within him after his last deployment, then I was all for it. Whatever kept him here with us.

I clapped a reassuring hand on his shoulder, and then we both got in our respective vehicles and drove away.

Chapter Twenty-Three

L eah

I HAD JUST CLOSED UP THE BOOKSTORE AND WAS ABOUT to meet Deacon at the diner down the street for dinner when someone came up behind me and slammed me face-first into the glass door of the store.

I couldn't see their face in the reflection through the glass, just that they had their hood pulled up and what looked and felt like a gun aimed at the side of my head.

"Please," I sobbed, holding my hands up. "Take whatever you want."

The man leaned in until his body was practically pressed against mine. When he spoke, his voice sounded familiar, but I was too terrified to pin it.

"We don't want anything. Yet. This is just a reminder that we can find you wherever you go. Even when you're playing house. Pay back the drugs, or the next time, this won't end so pleasantly for you."

"I don't have your drugs. I haven't scored in months," I said, my voice shaky.

He scoffed. "You think I'm stupid, bitch? You and Skeet better have my money the next time I see you."

I'd been about to tell him I had no idea who he was, but just as soon as he appeared, he was gone again. Even though the reflection confirmed that I was alone again, I still stood facing the door for several more minutes.

My hands shook as I lowered them and covered my mouth, hoping the bile that had started making its way up my throat wouldn't go any further.

I thought I had been done with that life when I left the hospital with Deacon after my last OD, but I guessed not.

Soon the bile and feeling of being scared were replaced by anger. How dare he drag me into business I had no part in. I briefly wondered if this was payback for leaving them behind after I got clean but shook off the thought. Even if he and Mav had been angry, that was no excuse to drag me into this bullshit.

I pulled myself together as much as I could and wiped the tears from my face before I continued down the sidewalk in the direction of the diner. Tomorrow, I would deal with Skeet. Tonight, I just wanted to have dinner with my boyfriend and curl up in his arms until the weight of the masked man at my back disappeared.

The next morning after Deacon left for work, I walked down to the bus stop and jumped on the one heading downtown. All through dinner last night, I couldn't shake the building anger at what Skeet had done. Really, I shouldn't have been surprised. It was the kind of thing I almost expected from him, but not from Mav.

I had hoped that Maverick had nothing to do with that man knowing my name, but I had no way of truly knowing if he had. I tried not to think about it too much or risk being disappointed when the truth came out. And it would come out today.

Thirty-five minutes later, the bus pulled into the downtown stop, and I got off. Nerves knotted my stomach from being back down here. I couldn't avoid downtown forever, but I wished I was back at our apartment right now.

I pulled the hood of my sweater up as I walked the familiar route to tent city. It was bittersweet being down here again. I was grateful for the home and family these streets had afforded me for so long, but I was also grateful for the chance to move on.

I came to an abrupt stop just outside the gate when I spotted the tent that used to be mine still in the same spot. It had a different occupant now, like was to be expected when someone abandoned theirs.

Nobody paid me any mind as I trudged through the small community. Pops sat outside his tent, rolling papers in his dirt-stained hands. He looked even skinnier than the last time I saw him. I cursed myself for not thinking ahead and bringing a few sandwiches with me. Once I was done having a conversation with Skeet and Mav, I would go to the nearest fast-food joint and get several burgers and pop to bring back here.

"Hiya, Pops," I said, voice shakes as I slipped my hands into my pockets. It was a chilly morning for being the middle of the summer. We were expecting rain today. I hoped it held off until later this afternoon.

"Well, look what the cat dragged in. How ya doing, Angel?" Pops said in between bouts of haggard coughing.

My heart ached every time I saw him deteriorate. I wondered if I could convince Deacon to help get Pops in to see a doctor. Although, I knew Pops would vehemently refuse. I still had to try, though. I wouldn't have been able to forgive myself if I had the means to help now and didn't.

"How ya doing, old man?" I kicked a piece of dirt with the toe of my sneaker and grinned when he scowled up at me.

"Now I know you not talking 'bout me."

"I wouldn't dare," I mock gasped and took a seat beside him, gently knocking shoulders with him.

"Mhm," he replied, turning his attention back to his task. "Missed you round these parts. Heard you got yourself a new man."

I brought my knees up to my chest and folded my arms around my legs.

"Deacon. He's… nice." I cringed at the word, but I didn't know how else to describe the man I'd fallen in love with without going into the specifics of why and what he'd done for me.

Pops snorted. "Sounds like he's more than just that."

I shrugged. "It's complicated."

And it was. As much as I believed I loved him, I didn't know who I was apart from the person I'd become after he saved my life and the ex-addict before. I felt like my life could be separated in two. Before Deacon and with Deacon. Three if I counted before, during, and after drugs.

I was young when I tried heroin for the first time. So young that I didn't remember who that person was. It went without saying that I wasn't exactly proud of the person I'd been while I was using. And now? Well, now I was even more confused.

Would Deacon and I ever be on equal footing if I always felt like I owed him?

"It always is," Pops said, putting the smoke between his lips and lighting it.

"You seen Skeet or Mav around today?"

"Saw Maverick at the Mission this morning. Skeet." Pops shook his head and breathed out a cloud of smoke. "That boy's going to get himself in deep shit if he doesn't quit."

My brows drew down in a frown. "He wasn't with Mav?"

The two of them were near inseparable since they got together years ago. It was odd that Skeet wouldn't be with Mav and vice versa.

"Nah," Pops said. "Mav's getting wiser. Noticing things about Skeet that don't add up."

Interesting.

As much as I would've liked spending the day chatting with Pops and catching up on all the goings-on around here, I had to talk to Skeet and get back home before Deacon was done work. I'd promised him I'd make his favourite meal today, and I wanted to make sure I had plenty of time to do just that. Plus, the longer I stayed down here the harder it was to refrain from falling back into old habits.

I stood up. "Thanks, old man," I teased.

Pops grunted but didn't bother with a reply; he knew I was kidding. I left tent city and made my way over to the Mission. It'd been getting closer to the time they started serving lunch. I hoped that Mav would still be there and that Skeet would join him soon if he hadn't already.

Mav and Skeet weren't at the Mission. It was getting late. I decided I'd try again tomorrow and was making my way back to the bus station when I saw them sitting outside the abandoned building of an old club about a block away from where I caught the bus.

"What the shit? Angel!" Mav grinned and grabbed my shoulders, pulling me into a bear hug. "How ya been, girl?"

Skeet grunted, taking a drag of his cigarette. "Look at her. New duds, new apartment, new dude. How'd you think she's doing? Living the high life. Right, Angel?"

Mav looked apologetic as he let me go and took a step back.

"Nice to see you too, Skeet," I said, raising a brow.

All the years I'd known him, and this was the first I'd seen this side of him.

"What ya doing back down here, Angel?" Mav asked. He remained standing between Skeet and me, and I thought it was telling that he hadn't stepped back beside his man.

Pops was right. Things seemed to be changing between the pair, and I wondered what had caused it.

"I had a visitor yesterday. A man I hadn't seen before." I looked directly at Skeet as I spoke. "He said I owed him for the drugs you and I took from him."

A choked sound came from Mav, but I didn't take my

eyes from Skeet, who looked unconcerned, almost bored.

"The thing is, I've never met this man in my life, nor have I taken any drugs from him. What have you gotten me involved in, Skeet?" I demanded.

He shrugged, toeing out his cigarette on the sidewalk. "Nothing your new sugar daddy can't take care of."

"Skeet! What the fuck?" Mav said. He sounded as mad as I felt, maybe more so.

Skeet rolled his eyes. "Fucking relax. I needed extra time, so I stalled. I'll take care of it."

Somehow, I didn't believe him, but we'd started gaining the attention of people around us. The last thing I wanted or needed was word to get out about this. So, I dropped it.

"You better" was all I said in response. "I need to go catch my bus."

"I'll walk you," Mav offered, ever the gentleman.

"Look," he said when we got to the station. My bus hadn't arrived yet, so we stood under the shelter. "I'll talk to Skeet again and get him to straighten things out, but —" He paused and shuffled his feet, suddenly looking uncomfortable as more people began to arrive for the bus. "You might not want to come down here by yourself again."

I laughed, but it wasn't with humour. "I remember what it's like, Mav. I haven't been gone that long."

He nodded; his eyes searched the crowd. "It's not safe down here for you anymore, Angel. I'll do my best with Skeet, but you need to stay away."

He turned and made his way through the crowd back to the abandoned building where Skeet waited.

What the hell was that about?

Chapter Twenty-Four

D eacon

THE LOCATION THE NON-PROFIT COMPANY HAD RENTED out for this fundraiser was a ballroom in an old hotel in the heart of downtown. The fact that they'd been able to rent it out in the middle of summer — tourist season — said a lot about how the company was doing *or* the kind of image they wanted to project to the rest of the community.

I hated these things. I got that they needed to raise money somehow, but did it really have to be with a fancy dinner catered to Adelaide and Vancouver's rich? It just seemed like a way to make these people feel good about themselves for donating to *charity*. I hated it. Maybe even more so now that I'd gotten to know personally one of the people these things were supposed to help. The only reason my family got invited to these was because my dad had been a lawyer for the city for almost twenty-seven years.

Supposed to.

A month or so ago, Leah had asked me if I'd go somewhere with her. Naturally, I'd agreed. Anything to spend more time with my girl. I drove, following her directions to a local shelter. This one was different from the one I'd volunteered at in the past. I had been uneasy at first, not sure if she'd meant to bring me here. I had told her from the start that I wanted to get to know her. All of her. That included her past, and I meant it. She silently grabbed my hand when we exited the truck and led me through the front door. I found out a couple of minutes later that we were there to volunteer for the afternoon. We did everything from playing cards with the residents to helping with coffee and going through the donation bin when requests came in. I realized then that what these fundraisers did wasn't enough. It barely scratched the surface.

I tried to push that day away for now and enjoy my date since we were here whether or not either of us wanted to be. My jaw had practically hit the floor when Leah emerged from the bedroom an hour ago wearing an emerald-green, floor-length dress my sister had lent her. The dress hugged her filled-out frame and showed off her curves. I would have a hell of a time keeping my hands to myself tonight. Her long hair was down in soft waves around her shoulders. I swept it to one side as we entered the dance floor, then pulled her closer with the press of a hand at the small of her back.

Leah beamed up at me, her smile bright and her eyes the happiest I'd seen since I met her. She placed a hand in one of mine and the other on my shoulder just like I'd shown her the first time we danced together. We moved around the floor effortlessly, like we had been dancing together our whole lives instead of only several months.

She laughed, the light sound tugging at my heart, when I spun her out and then back again, dipping her briefly, then bringing her up before continuing around the floor.

"I love you."

I closed my eyes and pressed our foreheads together. Our dancing had slowed to a gentle sway as I held her, breath caught in my chest.

"Are you sure?" Her voice was low so that only I could hear her. She glanced up at me, her brown eyes ping-ponging back and forth between mine as hope flared in hers. Even though we've said it before, it tore at something inside of me that she still questioned my feelings for her.

I chuckled. "I couldn't be more sure. You don't have to say anything now. I'll wait for as long as it takes to make you believe me."

She stopped swaying then. Her hand moved from my shoulder into the hair at the nape of my neck. "You won't have to wait long," she said.

I grinned wide then and kissed her in the middle of the dance floor, not caring the slightest bit who saw. The song changed, and I started swaying us again to the slow beat.

Leah and I danced for the next two songs after that before they announced that dinner would be served in five minutes. We found our table easily, and I pulled out her seat for her as my parents greeted us. Lilah arrived then too with her husband. It was a rare night when they could get a babysitter so that they both could come out.

Dinner wasn't bad. The portions were tiny, but I didn't expect anything different. My family included

Leah in their conversations like she'd been a part of us for so long. She seemed as taken with them as they were with her. Especially Lilah.

Leah was still a little reserved around my mom, but that was to be expected given her experiences. Mom took it all in stride too, staying back a bit to give Leah space if she needed. She said she understood that it wasn't personal and that she'd be there whenever Leah was ready to form some sort of friendship.

Before dessert was served, I excused myself to the bathroom. I also wanted to check in on Van and see how he was doing. I hadn't heard from him since the football game, and my big-brother senses were beginning to go off.

I'd just come out of the bathroom and was looking down at my phone when I caught a pair of heels coming to stop in front of me. I groaned internally and cursed myself for not being better prepared. I should've known she would be at one of these.

"Chloe," I said in greeting, not wanting to be a giant asshole.

"Deacon. Why haven't you returned any of my calls?" she whined in that nasal voice she knew I hated.

"I didn't think I should out of respect for my girlfriend and your fiancé, considering they were vastly inappropriate."

She rolled her eyes. "Speaking of which. Great job on your pet project. She's really come a long way."

"What the hell are you talking about?"

Chloe tilted her head to the side. Her gaze assessing. "That woman who entered your apartment while we were trying to reconcile." She giggled and stepped forward. "I have to admit that at first I was concerned, but I totally get it now."

"Leah was never a pet project, and we were not reconciling. You're engaged, Chloe. Nothing will ever happen between us again."

I ground my molars in an effort to stop myself from doing or saying something I'd regret later when she laughed like I said something funny. Chloe said something else as she took another step closer and fingered my tie, the backs of her fingers grazing against my chest. I hadn't heard a word she said because the announcer was back up on stage to let everyone know the auction would be starting in a few minutes. I had to get back to Leah; I'd already been gone longer than I wanted. But then something she said gave me pause.

"What did you just say? About Leah?"

She grinned, triumphantly, like she just won an award. "I asked if she told you how she likes to be shared? Apparently, your little project likes to be passed around to anyone with a dick. Acts like she doesn't want it too." Chloe scoffed and rolled her eyes. "It's kind of pathetic if you ask me."

I growled and her eyes grew wide as I backed her into the wall across from the bathrooms and loomed over her. I've never hit a woman. Was raised to never raise a hand to one, regardless of what profanities spewed from their lips, but Chloe seriously tested my patience. Especially now.

"If I ever hear Leah's name or anything to do with her coming out of your mouth —"

"What? You're going to hit me?"

I smirked. "No."

Chloe relaxed, a smile curling the corners of her painted lips. She reached out a manicured hand to touch me again but froze at my next words.

"I'll have a conversation with your fiancé and your

father. I'm sure the both of them would love to know about your extracurricular activities. I don't suppose your father would be so willing to hand over the company reigns then. Nor would your fiancé want to marry a cheating bitch."

"You wouldn't." Her eyes narrowed like if she tried hard enough she could call my bluff.

She wouldn't be able to because I wasn't fucking bluffing. She crossed a line tonight. Those things she spewed about Leah might have been true but that didn't give her the right to voice them. That right belonged to Leah and only Leah, and only when or if she was ready to share it. I knew Leah had a past. I also knew that I didn't know everything that had happened for to get to where she was. I'd hoped that she would be comfortable enough to share her whole story with me one day, but I also realized how much pain came with it so I wouldn't push. Frankly, if she never told me, I would be okay with that too. It was her choice.

"Deacon, please," Chloe whined.

"No," I said taking a step back. "This petty shit ends tonight."

I took another step back then turned and left, not bothering with a goodbye as I made my way back to the table. Both Leah and Lilah were gone when I made it back.

"Where'd they go?" I asked my parents. I could see Travis walking amongst the tables that held the auctioned items one last time before the bids were closed. Lilah couldn't be far then.

"She left, Deacon," Dad answered, his voice sounding unimpressed as he looked at me, something similar to disappointment in his eyes that looked so much like mine. People often mistook us for twins with how alike we looked.

"Lilah took her home. She looked like she'd been crying when she came back from the bathroom."

I cocked my head to the side. The men's and women's bathrooms were beside each other on this floor, and I didn't think I saw her when I came out. I froze. No. There was no way she'd overheard my conversation with Chloe. I didn't see anyone come around the corner; then again, we weren't exactly being quiet. Anybody could've heard our conversation through the wall.

Fuck.

I needed to find Leah. If she had overheard our conversation, then I needed to reassure her that I didn't give a shit. Her past was her past. I meant what I told her. I'd never judge her.

I bid my parents and Travis goodbye, agreeing to meet Travis for golfing next week, and then raced out of the ballroom and then the hotel. It felt like it took the valet a million fucking years to retrieve my truck. I tried calling her phone multiple times on the drive from the hotel to our apartment. There was no answer.

When I got back to the apartment, Leah wasn't there.

Chapter Twenty-Five

L eah

"Great job on your pet project. She's really come a long way."

Chloe's words rang in my ears as I rode the elevator up to our place. Deacon's. Deacon's place. It wasn't ours anymore, if it even had been in the first place. I knew enough now that I shouldn't take what came out of Deacon's ex's mouth as truth.

But I heard what she said next, and I wanted to die right there. My worst fear had come true. Deacon knew. The veil had been ripped away and he learnt about my demons.

"Apparently, your little project likes to be passed around to anyone with a dick. Acts like she doesn't want it too."

I thought I was going to be sick. The sad part was, I had planned on telling him about my past tonight after the dinner. The one thing I thought I could do right and I still failed.

I didn't even know if he'd still want me around after that. I mean, could I blame the guy for not wanting to date an addict? No. But it didn't mean that it didn't hurt like hell. It also reiterated my thoughts that I needed to find out if I could stand on my own without any help from him.

Chloe got one thing wrong, though. I didn't want it. Any of it. Not the way I lost my virginity and not the way I passed around to all his friends. Didn't meant that I still didn't feel dirty for what happened. That I didn't try to scrub off another layer of skin every time I showered, even twelve years later. I wasn't an addict when I first lived on the streets, but after that night it was inevitable. I needed the oblivion that heroin promised just so that I could forget their faces and the sounds they made. Deacon was the first man I'd ever willingly gave my body too, and he just might be the last.

I would forever be grateful that he had found me and offered to help me get clean, but that's where it should have ended. A relationship that started out like ours had no equal foundation. If I didn't walk away now and try to build a life on my own, I would always feel like I was indebted to him. That was no way to build a relationship.

Deacon looked ragged when I walked into the apartment the next morning to get a change of clothes. His short hair looked mussed, like he'd been running his fingers through it since last night. There were bags under his eyes that spoke of a restless night, and he looked like he had been in the middle of pacing the length of the apartment.

"Thank fuck," he said the minute he laid eyes on me.

He pulled me into his arms, and I let him, needing the contact as much as he did. But after a few heartbeats, I took a step back and then another and another until I was sure that enough space separated us that I wouldn't be tempted to reach for him.

"I'm not staying," I said and swallowed around a dry throat. "I just came to get my things."

"Leah, please," he pleaded. "I'm not sure what all you heard, but tell me how to fix it and do it. Just don't leave."

I choked on a sob and had to look away at his pained expression. I promised myself I wouldn't do this. I needed to get my things and leave. Anna was waiting downstairs for me. She'd offered to come up, but I needed to do this on my own. I couldn't keep relying on people. I had no idea what I would do now, but I was confident that I would figure it out because there was no other option.

I tried to get the words passed my lips to tell him that I didn't know how he still wanted me after learning that I was dirty. With tears streaming down my cheeks, I rushed down the hall toward Deacon's bedroom. I'd stopped sleeping in the guest room the first night we slept together. I found an old suitcase and started dumping a few changes of clothes in it. I'd get Lilah to return the suitcase to him once I had figured out my living situation. I may have also slipped one of his old T-shirts into the suitcase too, but I wasn't going to dwell on the reasons why just yet.

Deacon was in the same spot he'd been in when I started packing. I'd been tempted to move past him and walk out, but something stopped me. I stepped in front of him and tried to ignore the way my heart pulled me toward him.

"Answer me one thing," I said, my voice roughed up from a night of crying.

"Anything," he breathed.

"When you rescued me in that alley, was I just supposed to be a project for that non-profit?"

I held my breath as I waited for his answer. When minutes ticked by and all he'd done was blink at me as his face twisted in pain and regret, I swallowed down my tears and nodded briefly. That was all the answer I needed.

"Goodbye, Deacon."

With those parting words, I made myself walk away from the first man I'd ever truly given my heart to, and the first man to ever break it.

Chapter Twenty-Six

D eacon

My heart and my brain screamed at me to say something. Anything to stop her from walking out the front door. Instead, I stood there like an idiot. Silent. And watched the woman I loved walk away. Maybe I'd had it wrong all this time. Despite her words, maybe she didn't feel as much for me as I felt for her.

I didn't fight for her. I didn't argue that being with her felt righter than anything in my entire life. I didn't admit that as soon as Chloe spewed that shit, I shut it down fast. What had been the point? She was too upset to listen.

I didn't care that when Leah and I first met, she was homeless and addicted to heroin. I didn't care that the first time we spent any time together, she was so sick. Or that maybe she had multiple partners at one point. None of it mattered to me.

Anger replaced the despair that had begun taking hold. If she'd lied about being in love with me then she was going to fucking say it to my face. She was going to look me in the eye and tell me that it had all been a lie. I felt that hard to believe, though. After everything we'd been through together... there was no way that someone could fake that. I refused to believe it.

The ding of the elevator doors closing brought me out of my stupor, and I glanced around the empty apartment. She'd only just left, but already the apartment felt too quiet, too empty without her.

I didn't give a second thought to what I did next. I shoved my feet into the first pair of shoes I could find and grabbed my keys from the hook. I bypassed the elevator and took the stairs, hoping with everything I had that I wasn't too late.

Leah had spent her entire life believing that she wasn't worth fighting for, and I wasn't about to add my name to that list.

I broke into the lobby in a sprint and raced for the glass doors. I stopped just outside the building and looked left and right, trying to see if I could spot her. There was nobody at the bus stop, the one right outside or the one across the street, and the sidewalks were empty enough that I knew I should've been able to spot her instantly.

Not knowing what else to do, I pulled my phone from my pocket and jogged around the side of the building to the parking garage.

"D," my sister answered after what felt like an eternity.

"Where is she?"

Lilah sighed, and my heart dropped. I knew that sigh. I'd heard it a time or two while we'd been growing up. Lilah was fiercely loyal, and she wouldn't, under any circumstance — even to her own family — betray the trust of a close friend. It had put some of us in awkward positions in the past, but I loved her all the more for it.

"I'm sorry, Deacon. I promised."

"Delilah."

"I can't." She paused, and the silence stretched thick and long. "She needs time."

"How long? A day? two? She has a shift at the bookstore in two days."

My sister's voice turned hard when she said, "Do not go seeking her out. I mean it, Deacon. Give her time." She went quiet again, but when she spoke next, her voice was calm and full of sympathy. "If you don't give her this now, you could risk losing her forever."

I slumped back against the driver's seat of my truck. My knuckles turned white from where I had a death grip on the steering wheel to keep me from doing exactly what my sister had just asked me not to do.

"I've already lost her." I gave voice to the sinking feeling in my gut.

"No, you haven't. Just know that she doesn't blame you," Lilah added and then hung up.

I fought against all my instincts that said to go find her and bring her back here. Lilah was right. If I didn't respect Leah's wishes now, I could risk losing her, and that wasn't something I was willing to do. Now or ever.

So, I'd give her this because the alternative wasn't something I wanted to think about.

. . .

The End... for now. Book 2 coming later this year.

Trigger Warnings

Homelessness
- Drug use (on page)
- Drug withdrawals
- Mention of SA

About the Author

A.J. Daniels is now writing as *Andréa Joy*.

Andréa is a shark obsessed, beach loving, South African girl forced to endure the long Canadian winters for the last twenty-one years. She's currently trying to convince her husband that they should move somewhere tropical, but it's a work in progress. Fingers crossed, though!

When she's not writing or at her big girl job, you can find her binge-watching true crime shows, Bones, 911 Lone Star, or Friends, or hiding away with a good book. Coffee and chocolate are her love languages.

Feel free to check out her website or stalk her on social media.

www.authorandreajoy.com

Also by Andréa Joy

Famiglia Series (Mafia)

Dark Desire (M/F)

Dark Betrayal (M/F)

Deadly Intentions - Novella

Dark Illusion (M/M)

Deadly Surrender - Novella

A Famiglia Christmas - Novella

Bound to You - Novella

Dark Obsession (M/F)

De Luca Famiglia Boxset

The Fallen Duet (Paranormal Reverse Harem with M/M+)

Cursed

Redeemed

Twist of Fate Series (Contemporary)

Then There Was You (M/F)

COMING SOON

The Rutherford Family Series

Donovan

Dash

Damien

Drake

The Famiglia Series Next Gen

Il Diavolo (M/M)

Made in the USA
Middletown, DE
26 April 2022